my NOT-SO-GREAT French Escape

my NOT-SO-GREAT French Escape

CLIFF BURKE

CLARION BOOKS
An Imprint of HarperCollinsPublishers

Clarion Books is an imprint of HarperCollins Publishers.

My Not-So-Great French Escape
Copyright © 2023 by Cliff Burke
All rights reserved. Printed in the United States of America. No part of this book may be used or reproduced in any manner whatsoever without written permission except in the case of brief quotations embodied in critical articles and reviews. For information address HarperCollins Children's Books, a division of HarperCollins Publishers, 195 Broadway, New York, NY 10007.
www.harpercollinschildrens.com

Library of Congress Cataloging-in-Publication Data
Names: Burke, Cliff, author.
Title: My not-so-great French escape / Cliff Burke.
Description: First edition. | New York, NY : Clarion Books, [2023] | Audience: Ages 8–12. | Audience: Grades 4–6. | Summary: Hoping to reconnect with his best friend, Rylan accompanies him on a month-long stay at a working farm in France, where he navigates new friendships and anticipates meeting his estranged father.
Identifiers: LCCN 2022014387 | ISBN 9780358701507 (hardcover)
Subjects: CYAC: Farm life—Fiction. | Friendship—Fiction. | France—Fiction. | LCGFT: Novels.
Classification: LCC PZ7.1.B8774 My 2023 | DDC [Fic]—dc23
LC record available at https://lccn.loc.gov/2022014387

Typography by Celeste Knudsen
23 24 25 26 27 LBC 5 4 3 2 1

First Edition

For my students, especially for those
who feel like they do not belong

There is nothing better than the encouragement of a good friend.

—Jean-Jacques Rousseau

ONE

"Smile!" my mom urged.

I was standing in front of a pulled-down white screen in the corner of a CVS as a harried cashier struggled with an old digital camera.

"He's actually not allowed to smile," the cashier corrected.

I let my face fall into a grimace.

"You also can't frown," the cashier said. "You just have to look normal."

"I'm trying to look normal," I said, doing my best to keep my face absolutely blank.

The cashier shrugged. "It's *your* passport picture." He clicked the silver button and passed the camera over for Mom's inspection.

She glanced disapprovingly and asked, "Would you mind taking another?"

"This isn't a photo shoot," the cashier said.

"I know, I'm sorry. Just *one* more."

"Fine. Last one." He readjusted the focus on my face.

"A *liiitttlle* smile," Mom begged.

"But don't smile," the cashier said.

I tried to smile without smiling while also looking normal. In the small picture printed and handed to me, I looked like I was angrily holding in a yawn.

We left the store, and I trudged to the passenger side of Mom's car. For the past two years the door wouldn't budge unless popped open from the inside. As I waited for her to open it, I inspected my passport photo again, hoping it might look different in the sunlight. It didn't.

"That wasn't so bad, was it?" Mom said once I slid into my seat.

"I look like I'm sick."

"I think you look handsome. Maybe a little confused, but still handsome. Besides, your passport won't last forever."

"How long does it last?"

"Ten years."

I gulped as I envisioned still carrying this awful picture around at twenty-two.

"Can we maybe go to another CVS?" I asked.

"No." She plucked the picture from my hands and examined it again. "It really isn't so bad."

She handed it back to me, and I turned it facedown on my lap.

"You know, I didn't have *my* first passport until I was twenty-five," she said.

"I *know*, Mom." She'd been repeating this tidbit for the past four weeks.

"And I didn't go to France until I was thirty-two."

"I. Know."

"Why do you get so upset when I try to share the details of my life?"

"Because you share the same details over and over."

"We can't all live such fascinating lives. You're just lucky Serena still likes me."

I also knew I was lucky. Serena was Mom's best friend from college, and she had become extremely rich by creating an app that reminded other rich people to drink water. They used to forget, apparently, but are now very well hydrated and Serena is very well paid. So well paid that for the past year she's "sponsored" my education at the St. Dominic de Guzman School for Sterling Scholars in Menlo Park, California.

"And that Wilder still likes *you*," Mom said.

"I don't know about that," I said.

"He asked you to come with him, didn't he? He could have asked anyone."

"I'm sure you had nothing to do with that."

"*Rylan*, I didn't say anything about him bringing you. When was the last time I even saw him?"

"And you didn't mention anything to Serena?"

"A suggestion here or there, maybe. But certainly not what you're implying."

"Sure," I said.

"Besides, I thought you guys made up."

"I guess. But that doesn't mean there aren't, what's the word, *repercussions*."

"One of which is that he's trying to make it up to you by *inviting you to France*." She danced around in her seat in an imitation of a mime or a French person or something.

"What are you doing?"

"This is the French *yé-yé* girl dance," she said. "You didn't think your mom knew about *yé-yé*."

"I have no idea what that means, so no, it's not surprising."

"Add it to your list."

"How many things do I have to read before I leave? I thought the point was to discover the culture *there*."

"Yes, but you don't want to be uncultured beforehand. The French don't take kindly to that."

"From what I've read, they don't take kindly to most things."

"That's not true. They love things that are French."

I pulled out my phone and added "*yé-yé*" to my *French Things Mom Says I Need to Know* Notes document, below "Jean-Luc Godard" and "coq au vin."

"What's coke ah vin, again?" I asked.

"*Coq. Au. Vin,*" she enunciated. "Chicken in wine sauce. You'll probably have that at the farm."

"You think he's going to give us wine?"

"Wine *sauce.* You wouldn't get drunk from it. Unless you ate the entire chicken."

"Why would I eat an entire chicken?"

"You're a growing boy," she said. "I wouldn't be surprised if he served wine, too."

"*Really?!*" I said excitedly.

"It's a French custom. But just a few sips, hopefully."

"Or a few glasses."

"He wouldn't do that. Right?"

"How would I know?"

"Pierre's the first person on the list," she said. "Please tell me you've read at least a little about him."

Pierre de Beaulieu was the owner of the French farm where Wilder and I would be staying and working for the next month, and I'd read more than a little about him. I knew that his great-great uncle was a famous general who protected Napoleon from an attempted assassination. That as a reward for taking a bullet in his cheek, this uncle was gifted a château in northern France. That after a century of neglect, Pierre moved back to the château and began the process of converting it into a fully organic farm. And that when he grew tired of paying people, he started inviting students to work for free through a program called SCOFF: Students Communing on French Farms.

But, while there were many glowing reviews of the SCOFF program online, there weren't any mentions of Pierre's farm, his personality, or whether or not he served wine with dinner.

TWO

Against my wishes, we went directly from CVS to Wilder's house. He used to live in Belmont, five minutes away from us, but his house was now a twenty-five-minute drive into the manicured greens and gated complexes of Atherton.

"*Bienvenue*," Serena said as she opened their thick front door.

"*Merci*," Mom said with a giggle.

They greeted each other French style: gently touching cheeks while puckering their lips and making a kissing sound.

"Come here, Rylan," Serena said, leaning down slightly. "You must practice *faire la bise*." She pressed her right cheek to mine and made a kissing sound while I tried to do the same. But mine sounded more like a mouth fart, and Serena recoiled.

"Wilder's in his room," she said flatly.

I stepped past her and waved to Wilder's dad, who was working on his laptop at the kitchen table. Though he spoke within a limited range of expressions, he was always nice to me. I was expecting a "There he is," but was surprised with a "There's our guy."

He followed that up with "Doing good?"

"Yep."

"Well, all right."

I knew that was the end of our conversation, so I walked up the stairs, past the painted portrait of Wilder, where he's posed like an angel, and stopped at his bedroom door. I considered knocking but instead swung it open and said, "What. Up" in a robot voice.

He was sprawled on his bed, rapidly texting, and he barely looked up. "One second," he mumbled.

I immediately felt foolish. I rolled out his desk chair and spun in slow circles, waiting for Wilder's attention. He continued tapping his thumbs without looking at me.

I pulled out my phone and texted him, "hey man."

He made an irritated *tsk* sound as my text flashed on his phone. "This is important," he said.

"Can I use your computer, then?" I asked.

"No."

I turned anyway and tried to type in his old password, but it didn't work.

I sighed and inspected the corkboard of pictures that hung next to his desk, surprised to find one picture of us remaining in the far-left corner. It was from the first day of kindergarten, when we were still best friends.

We had first met as toddlers, when our moms plopped us next to each other and asked that we share toys. He had better toys than I did and wasn't very good at sharing, but over time, when I learned that crying and shouting "He won't share" isn't the best way to make friends, we formed a bond.

By the time we entered kindergarten and could decide who to sit next to, we chose each other. The teacher tried to encourage us to make new friends, and even forbade us from sitting together, but her plan didn't work. We sat a space apart, ducked our heads behind the person between us, and kept on talking until our teacher changed her policy.

This continued until fifth grade, when Serena started making money and pulled Wilder out of public school. For the first few months, we still spent weekends together, but soon he was invited to sleepovers at mansions and parties at backyard pools. I became self-conscious whenever he came to my apartment and embarrassed when we climbed into our apartment complex's small shared pool, knowing that splashing around a twenty-foot circle must be disappointing after swimming laps in luxury.

We still hung out on special occasions, always at Wilder's house, but by the end of the school year we were more like cousins than best friends. Which is why I was so surprised when Mom told me that starting in sixth grade, I'd be going to the same private middle school as Wilder. I protested, but Mom wouldn't budge. It would be fine, she said. I would have Wilder, she said. He still *was* my best friend. We had just spent a little time apart.

But she was wrong.

At the St. Dominic de Guzman School for Sterling Scholars, every student is given their own laptop and Google account. While everyone appears "sterling" on the surface, their true personalities are expressed in hundreds of privately shared Docs and Slides. There, everyone competes to find the most offensive memes and savagely bullies one another.

At the beginning of the year, I was shared on some of the meme Slides and praised for my contributions. I thought I was doing fairly well. In class, I was sought out as a partner for collaborative projects. I knew I was doing more than my fair share of the work, but I didn't let that fact bring me down. My teachers, in their page-long essays that served as "grades," described me as "curious and engaged" and only needing to grow in my "self-advocacy skills."

But after the first month or so, I felt a certain distance from everyone. Most of them had known each other since pre-K, and their tangled history with one another, their sense of being "real" Sterling Scholars who grew up together, created a barrier that was nearly impenetrable. Wilder had fit in because his greatest skill was molding himself to be liked by whomever was directly in front of him. He was not fully accepted, but he was certainly liked. The few times I was invited to a party outside of school, it was clearly due to respect for him, not because anyone really wanted me hanging around.

This was just a general feeling until two months ago, when Wilder accidentally shared a slideshow titled *Rylan*. There were pictures of crumbling shacks and bombed-out apartment complexes marked "Rylan's house," a homeless beggar woman marked "Rylan's mom," and a man running away from home marked "Rylan's dad."

I went into the version history to see who contributed. Nearly everyone in the grade had taken turns trying to find the worst pictures of poverty.

But worst of all was the last slide. Wilder was the only person who knew that my dad had left when I was three.

He knew that my mom had spent a year trying to get my dad to come back. He knew that I used to—and maybe sometimes still did—blame myself. And Wilder was the person who added the man running away from home.

I didn't tell any of the teachers, didn't advocate for myself as they had suggested. Instead, I added a new slide that said, "Thanks guys!" over a picture of a raging wildfire.

Wilder apologized and said it was all a joke. He was just trying to get the biggest reaction. He'd never meant for me to see it. Obviously, that was not how he saw me, or my house, or my mom, or my dad.

After a week I accepted his apology, but things were still weird between us. When we hung out now, it was mostly like this: him attending to others on his phone while I sat by his side.

"Okay, what's up," he said, finally finished with his "important" texts.

"Oh, not much, just sitting here waiting for you."

"Come on," he said. "Stop being so dramatic."

"It's fine," I said. "Keep texting."

He sighed. "Can we do a truce or something?"

"Can you answer a question first?"

He looked confused. "Yes?"

"And be honest."

He held his hand to his heart. "I'm always honest."

I asked the question that had swirled around my head over the past weeks: "Did your mom *make* you invite me?"

His hand minutely flinched from its place over his heart. "No . . ." he said unconvincingly. "I mean, not exactly."

"So yes."

"She *suggested* it. But I'm happy you're coming and everything," he said quickly while attempting a smile.

I glared at him.

"Who else would I invite?" he said.

I rattled off the names of six people whom he seemed to like more than me.

"They're fun to hang out with *at school*," he said.

"And at their houses," I said.

"They do have nice houses. And yes, sometimes they're fun. But it's not fun like how we used to have fun."

"Used to," I repeated.

"It's not like you've been asking *me* to hang out either," he said.

"Because you never want to," I said.

"Maybe I *would* want to if you didn't spend the whole time moping."

"I don't mope."

"You're currently moping." He took a picture of my face and handed me his phone. "See?"

I looked down at my scowling face and started to laugh. "This is more of a sulk," I said, and tossed his phone back.

"Sulk, mope, whatever you want to call it. That's what you've looked like."

"And this is what you've looked like." I held my phone in front of my face and pretended to text for thirty seconds.

"Stop," he said, laughing, dragging my arm down. "I get it."

It felt good to laugh with him again.

"So how about that truce?" Wilder asked. "For the rest of the summer, we're best friends again."

I looked into his eyes. I didn't know if he was being genuine or just trying to make the trip more pleasant. There were only so many ways to ignore me when we'd be sharing a room at a farm in a foreign country. But I wanted the next month to be fun, too, and maybe this would be our way back to being best friends again.

"Deal," I said.

THREE

Wilder and I hung out every day for the next two weeks, just the two of us. Without anyone else around to impress, he returned to his old self. Or I returned to my old self. Or maybe both of us hadn't really changed, it was only the social circles of school that had formed a wedge between us, then pulled us apart.

In preparation for the trip, we kept a steady schedule. We researched one of the items from my mom's list every morning and attended French language lessons at his dining room table with a college-age tutor every afternoon.

I had learned a lot of food vocabulary and several verbs, but still struggled to put sentences together. The one phrase

I had mastered was "The boy is eating an orange." When the moment arose, I was prepared to speak this sentence flawlessly.

With only two nights remaining before we left, I was at least confident in how much I had learned about French culture. I had listened to *yé-yé* and *chanson*, learned the history of the Eiffel Tower and Notre-Dame, and explored the many varieties of cheese found in northern France.

While I was revisiting the Google Images results for "most delicious French cheeses," Mom lightly knocked on my door. Before I could answer, she stepped into my room.

"Looking up some . . . pictures of cheese?"

"It's on the list," I said.

"Just Camembert was on the list," she said as she sat on my bed.

"I started there, but did you know there are over *one thousand* types of French cheese?"

"I've had at least seven."

"Only nine hundred ninety-three to go."

She smiled. "I hope you can try at least a hundred."

"The only thing I have left to research is"—I pulled out my phone to check the list—"May 1968."

"That's a big one," she said. "A bit more complicated than cheese."

"What is it? What happened?"

"You'll have to find out."

I spun my chair to search it up.

"But not right now," she said. "I have something more . . . pressing to tell you."

I swiveled my chair back around to face her. "Pressing?"

"Complicated," she clarified.

"Did Wilder drop out?"

She shook her head. "No. It has nothing to do with him. Why—are you not getting along?"

"No, we are."

"Well . . ." she started hesitantly. "This is about . . . It's your father."

I stared at her, dumbfounded.

She tried to smile, but it looked more like a wince. "He sent me a message."

"What do you mean?"

"He 'wants to get back in touch.' With me. Because he wants to get back in touch with you."

"I don't understand." I had never been in touch with him. Can't remember saying a word to him. He left before I could form complete sentences.

"It seems he lives in Paris."

I looked at her hands, which she twisted nervously.

"I mean, he does live in Paris," she said.

As far as I knew, she'd lost contact with him years ago.

He left when I was three, and not like when I was three and three-quarters, but the day after my third birthday party. There are pictures to prove that he was there, and none afterward. Since then, he has never called, emailed, written a letter, sent a birthday card. Mom always assured me that I had nothing to do with it. He had made a decision based on how they were doing at the time. She spent a year trying to get him to change his mind, but then she stopped and moved on. That was always the story, at least. I can't even remember the last time we talked about him.

"About six months ago he sent me an email," Mom said. "He just got married again and wants to *address his wrongdoings*."

"You don't believe him?" I asked.

"I don't know what to believe. He hasn't always been the most trustworthy person."

"But what did you say?"

"I didn't say anything."

"Why not?"

"Because it's not my—" She paused. "I don't have anything to say to him. But he did ask about you, and this *will* be a part of your life whether you . . ."

It all made sense now. Why Serena signed Wilder up for SCOFF. Why he invited me to join him. Why Mom insisted that I accept.

"And so you planned to trick me into meeting him," I said.

"*Honey*," she said gently. "I'm not trying to trick you."

"Then what are you trying to do?"

"I'm giving you an option. A possibility."

She gestured for me to join her on the bed. I reluctantly sat next to her.

"You don't have to talk to him or meet him or anything if you don't want to. But if you *do*, Serena booked a hotel for one extra day at the end of your trip. She can help you make arrangements."

"So this *is* a trick."

"I know it seems that way, but I promise this is not a trick. I want you to enjoy your time in France. *Really*. But I felt like I couldn't keep this from you." She took a slip of paper from her pocket and placed it on my knee. Written in her neat handwriting was my father's email address.

"You're old enough to decide whether or not you want to send him a message. If you want to, that's okay. If not, that's also okay." She squeezed my shoulder.

I folded the paper and put it in my pocket. "What would you do?" I asked.

She thought for a moment. "If I were in your situation . . . I'd probably want to meet him. He is your father, after all."

"So you *do* think I should meet him?"

"I trust you to make your own decision."

"And if I do meet him and like him, and want to—"

"You're moving a few steps ahead."

"You cut me off," I said.

"I don't want you to get your hopes up too high."

"What does that mean?"

"It means what it means."

"So, you don't think I should meet him?"

"I'm not going to tell you what to do."

"I wish you would."

"Do what feels right."

"I don't know what feels right."

"You can think about it. You have time."

I sighed and stared at my computer screen, wishing I could return to three minutes ago, when trying to find the most delicious French cheese was my greatest concern.

Mom wrapped her arms around me and whispered, "*Je t'aime, mon petit prince.*"

"I only know what half of that means," I said.

"It means 'I love you, my little prince.'"

FOUR

The slip of paper with my father's email was faceup on my desk when I awoke the next morning. I folded it into a small square and put it inside my top desk drawer. I had a lot of packing to do.

But as much as I tried to focus on taking out twelve pairs of underwear, fourteen pairs of socks, seven pairs of shorts, two pairs of jeans, and ten T-shirts I was willing to "become fragrant with dirt" (as Pierre had recommended), my mind kept circling back to the little square of paper that could end a decade of silence.

I often picture the events of my life like scenes in a movie. For as long as I can remember, my mom and I have gone to the movie theater every Monday night. There's a special discount where it costs only ten dollars for both of us, plus unlimited free popcorn. Because she's not strict about ratings, I've seen my fair share of PG-13 movies and even a few R-rated ones, though nothing that she deems too violent.

As I sorted through my clothes, my mind began to piece together the scene that would unfold if I emailed my father. His pocket would buzz, and he'd pull out his phone, his face brightening when he saw it wasn't a boring work email, but a message from his long-lost son.

He would take a moment to think, spinning in his stylish yet functional computer chair in his small but well-decorated Paris apartment, before pouring out his heart through his fingertips, apologizing for all the years he missed, assuring me how much he loved me, how happy he would be to meet me.

Then, the more realistic scene played out in my head. He reads my email without flinching, puts his phone back in his pocket, and decides to ignore it. He waits until he's sure I've left France and then responds to say he's so sorry he missed me, what a bad bit of luck, he hopes I might make it back sometime soon because he really would like to see me. He just lost track of time and I could understand how that goes, right?

As my mind wove narratives, I realized that the mental image of my father I was using was almost ten years old. It came from a picture of him at my third birthday party, sitting on an armchair with a slight smile, raising a slice of cake to the camera. I kept this picture underneath my bed alongside a box of DVDs he left behind, mostly cop dramas from the 1970s that I watched in secret whenever Mom was out of the house.

I tried to imagine what he would look like now— larger? thinner? bald? bearded?—but I couldn't settle on a clear image. I had obviously looked him up before but never had much luck. Michael O'Hare is a pretty common name, and the first results page was dominated by a TV actor from the '80s. The next page featured a popular chef named Metal Michael, who posted videos of himself head-banging behind a plate of food. Then there were a bunch of obituaries.

But now I had a new piece of intel. I searched "Michael O'Hare Paris" and found a pixelated picture that looked like an aged version of the photo under my bed. His hair had grayed and was a little longer, the lines in his face more pronounced. And he looked happy. Happier than he'd looked at my third birthday party. I tried to click and expand his photo, but it broke into distorted little dots.

I closed out and spun around in my chair. Having a more recent face to imprint on my visions of the future didn't make it any easier to write him an email.

I lugged Mom's black suitcase out from her closet and returned to Pierre's clothing list, carefully gathering what I didn't mind getting a little dirty, rolling them into what Mom called clothes burritos, and lining the bottom of the suitcase. Before I knew it, the suitcase was full. I sat on top of it like a horse jockey and wrestled the zipper into closing.

Then I went back to my desk, took out the piece of paper with my father's email address, and tucked it into the suitcase's front pocket.

I'd deal with it once I landed.

FIVE

Though Wilder had lobbied to travel without Serena, she decided it would be best to accompany us to Paris and ensure that we made it onto the correct train to the farm. This didn't bother me, as it meant that we'd be flying first class. I'd only been on one flight before and had spent the whole time squished between my mom and an elderly man who could not stop eating hard-boiled eggs.

As we were graciously welcomed into the first-class cabin, I knew I wouldn't need to fear any egg-eaters crowding my personal space. Everyone had their own little pod, with a large, cushioned seat, footrest, blanket, and laptop-size screen stocked with over five hundred movies.

"I don't hear any complaints now," Serena said as Wilder was led to his seat.

He glared at her, clamped his headphones over his ears, and mumbled something indecipherable.

"You don't treat your mother this way, do you?" she asked me.

"I try not to," I said as I was directed to my own pod behind Wilder.

"Order whatever you'd like," she said from across the aisle.

"*Anything?*" I flipped through the heavy leather menu.

"It's all taken care of," she said nonchalantly. "Now if you'll excuse me," she continued, removing a velvet sleep mask from a hidden compartment in the armrest, "I'm going to get some beauty rest. I get some of my best sleep in the sky."

As Serena slept and Wilder blasted music, I ate two doughnuts, French toast, scrambled eggs, sausage, bacon, a small package of roasted almonds, and a complimentary mint while watching three movies. It was a perfect morning. I secretly hoped we would circle in the air for a few more hours due to some slight, nonfatal flying error, but it wasn't meant to be. Exactly five hours later, we landed in the bustle of JFK Airport in New York City.

Serena led us from escalator to escalator; up, down, and across the airport as if it were her office building. After depositing us in the correct waiting area for the plane to Paris, she went to browse the mini bookstore, leaving Wilder and me alone for the first time.

"Finally." He exhaled, removing his headphones.

"You're talking now?" I said.

He rolled his eyes. "You know I don't like to talk when *she's* listening." He gestured dismissively toward his mom's luggage.

"She was asleep on the plane."

"I thought we made a truce," Wilder said, though he continued looking down at his phone.

"We *did*, but it seems like—"

"Whoa, did you see this?" Wilder interrupted.

"I'm still on airplane mode."

"It's from Pierre." Wilder waved me over.

The subject line read "Bienvenue à Château de Beaulieu!" and the message was a single word—*Enjoy*—followed by seven flower and heart emojis and a private video link. Wilder clicked the link, tilted his screen sideways, and we enjoyed.

It began with Pierre behind the wheel of a fancy, old-timey convertible, coasting down a tree-lined dirt road. His wavy graying hair flopped on both sides of his head as the scarf that was wrapped around his neck fluttered in the wind. The car stopped in front of an iron gate, which slowly opened to reveal a stately four-spired castle.

My jaw dropped. "I thought we were *farming*?"

"With a great pleasure, I welcome you to Château de Beaulieu," Pierre said in accented English. He stepped out of the car and whipped off his driving scarf. Under it he was wearing stained overalls. He was very tall and thin and looked more like a scarecrow than a farmer. "I am excited to be seeing all of the scoff-airs soon."

Wilder paused the video. "*Scoff airs*?"

"SCOFFers," I said. "You know, Students Communing on French Farms . . . ers."

Wilder hummed in agreement and pressed Play. There followed a rapid series of cuts as Pierre introduced the various farm activities:

"We have cherry picking." He held a basket of cherries in front of an entire forest of cherry trees.

"Milking the goat." He pumped two shots of milk from a goat's udder into a metal bucket and then whispered, "*Brava*" into the goat's ear.

"Make the roses nice." He leaned down and plucked a single weed from a manicured rose garden.

"Experiment with vegetables." He stepped through a densely overgrown garden that didn't appear to have any vegetables.

"Be friendly with the bees." Dressed in a spotless beekeeper outfit, Pierre lifted the lid off a wooden crate, and hundreds of bees swarmed his arms.

"Restore the old glass house." He stood in the center of an antique greenhouse made of small glass squares, more than half of which were missing.

"And, someday, retake the castle from the birds." He walked through the castle doors, and the camera tilted upward. Bird nests lined every rafter, and pigeons swooped from window to window.

Pierre returned to the front door of the castle and addressed the camera directly. "Our team this summer is filled with many *passionate* young people from France and the rest of the world. It is my hope that we can learn from each other and learn from nature. I will be seeing you soon." He winked, and the video ended.

Wilder and I stared at each other in disbelief.

"That's not what I was expecting," Wilder said.

"What were you expecting?" I asked.

"I don't know, more of, like, an Old MacDonald–style guy."

"I don't think French people say e-i-e-i-o."

Wilder laughed and put his phone back in his pocket. "I don't know about sleeping in the castle, but the rest does look pretty fun, I guess."

"I don't think we're sleeping in the castle," I said. "There was stuff dripping from the ceiling."

"You mean bird poop," Wilder said.

"Oh my god." I mentally replayed the end of the video and realized that Wilder was right. Bird poop was falling from the ceiling of the castle like white rain.

We were doubled over laughing when Serena came back with bottles of water. "Aw," she cooed, "look at you two. Having so much fun already."

"We're talking about bird poop," Wilder said.

"Well"—Serena winced—"whatever it takes to bond."

We started laughing again as Serena moved toward the forming line. She motioned for us to follow as the man at the gate announced first-class boarding for the flight to Paris.

SIX

The second plane ride went much the same as the first. Once we'd landed in Paris and collected our luggage, Serena shepherded us onto the RER, or regional express train. For the first time, Wilder was appreciative that his mom was with us. She knew which train transfer we'd need to safely arrive at the station in Dreux, where Pierre had promised to pick us up.

The train moved from below to above ground as we traveled into the center of Paris. It was eleven a.m., and the streets were bustling. I pressed my face to the window and inspected the face of each man that passed. Was it my father's Sunday-morning routine to visit a café by the metro? Was that him, stopping to buy flowers for his new wife? Or was he sitting at a table by himself, reading the newspaper?

As if sensing what I was doing, Serena laid a soothing hand on my shoulder.

"Remember that we have a day in Paris after your stay on the farm. You know, if you want to go on any *special trips*," she said unsubtly.

"Special trips?" Wilder puzzled.

"Just something to think about," she continued. "I can, of course, plan our Paris day, but if either of you, Rylan in particular, thinks of anything *you'd* like to do, just send me a message."

"Okay . . ." Wilder said.

I smiled weakly and mumbled, "Thank you. I'll, uh, think it over."

"Please do," she said. "Anything at all. I'm here to help."

"We get it, Mom," Wilder said.

The train came to a stop at Gare Montparnasse. Tearfully, Serena led us to the sliding doors of our final train to Dreux.

"Mom, *please*, relax," Wilder said, trying to shield himself from French onlookers.

"You'll [sniffle] let me know when you [sniffle] get there?" she whimpered.

"It's a forty-minute train ride," Wilder said.

"I'll email you," I said.

"Thank you." She cleared her tears with her fingertips. "I don't know why I'm getting so emotional. Come here." She wrapped herself around us, her arms stretching wide to rest on our backpacks. "I love you both so much. Enjoy your time on the farm."

She watched as we took our seats. Through the open window she shouted a teary *au revoir* as the train chugged out of the city and into the countryside.

We were the only people who exited the train at the Gare de Dreux. Pierre had promised to meet us at the station with a sign, but we found only a gurgling fountain, a fruit seller, and a woman sitting on her luggage, crying into her phone.

"Should we text him?" Wilder asked, immediately pulling out his phone. Mom had said that I wouldn't need an international plan as long as I regularly checked my email, but Wilder had opted for the full international phone package and was already receiving texts from California.

"I'm sure he's on his way," I said distractedly while trying to test out my French language abilities. I could understand that the fruit seller was calling out the names of fruit, and the woman on the phone kept repeating the word for love. But in a sad way.

"Then what should we do?" Wilder said.

"I don't know. Take . . . *this* . . . in." I waved my hands toward the fountain and the crying woman.

"Take *this* in." He rolled his luggage into my leg and went to ask the fruit seller if he sold chips.

As the fruit seller said "No, no, no po-ta-to" in the rhythm of a children's song, a rusty car pulled up. The glare of the sun against the windshield disguised the identity of the driver, but this was certainly not the antique convertible featured in Pierre's video.

Nevertheless, when the car came to an abrupt stop, the door creaked open, and Pierre unfolded himself from the driver's seat. He was even taller in person, his height elongated by the white beekeeper suit he wore. I waved as he strode toward me holding a large sign that read *Pierre*.

I awkwardly extended my hand. "Pierre, I take it."

"*Oui, oui,*" he said, launching the sign toward a trash can and batting my hand away. He leaned down for *faire la bise*. I managed to rub cheeks and make a dignified kiss sound without embarrassing myself.

"Which one are you?" he asked.

"Rylan," I said.

"Ah yes, Ree-lon," Pierre said, stretching my name into new shapes.

"And I'm Wilder," Wilder announced, walking back from the fruit seller with a plum.

"The wild man," Pierre said while doing a little swiveling hip dance. "Welcome, welcome. You can follow me. We have much to do."

We trailed him back to the car and carted our luggage to the trunk.

"The trunk, no," Pierre said. "It is off-limits."

"*Off-limits?*" I repeated.

"It is full," Pierre clarified. "With bees."

"Bees?!" we both exclaimed.

"Yes," he said nonchalantly. "The back seat is best for the bags."

I opened the door and discovered another white beekeeper suit laid along the back seat.

"Can I move this?" I asked.

"You could," Pierre said. "But it would be much better if you wear it."

"Will I get stung if I don't?" I asked.

"Not now, no," Pierre said.

"But later . . ."

"Soon, yes, you will need it."

"Because . . ."

"We are going to get more bees."

"I thought we didn't work on Sundays," Wilder said.

"This is not work, but pleasure," Pierre said.

Wilder and I looked at each other. He vehemently shook his head.

"I guess I'll do it," I said meekly.

"*Super!*" Pierre exclaimed.

I stepped into the white one-piece beekeeper suit and Pierre zipped up the back. Then we all climbed into the cramped car, Wilder and I with our feet resting on top of our bags. Pierre peeled out of the station and began talking animatedly about bees.

We passed through the small town of Dreux and into the narrow dirt roads of the woods. A neighbor of his, Pierre explained, was a professional beekeeper and had given him a tip about where to find the best bees.

"The bees in the back," Pierre continued, "are bad. Always angry. Not working together. This is why we are going to throw them away and get the good bees."

He slowed the car next to a small creek. "Are you ready, Ree-lon?" he asked into the rearview mirror.

I was not ready. But I was at least wearing a suit designed to prevent beestings. Wilder was wearing a T-shirt and shorts.

"Should I stay in the car?" Wilder asked.

"If you want to be boring," Pierre said, leaping out of

the car. "Come and wave the bad bees bye-bye."

"Could I at least get a sweater or something?" Wilder asked.

"The bees will not bite," Pierre said.

"They sting," Wilder said.

"Is possible," Pierre said, lowering his beekeeper helmet.

"Do I get one of those?" I asked.

"Of course." Pierre popped the trunk and handed me a veiled helmet and thick black gloves. He picked up a tin can with a spout on top and an accordion-style bag attached to one side. "You will be the smoker," he told me, squeezing the bag and releasing a huge puff of smoke.

I quickly dropped the helmet over my head, but not before the smoke hit my lungs.

"What [cough] do I [cough] do?" I asked.

"It is easy," Pierre said. He lifted a buzzing wooden box from the trunk and gently placed it ten feet from the car. "You send a little bit of smoke for the bees, and it gets them all"—he stirred his hands around, searching for the right English phrase—"*going crazy* because they think they are on fire. Then I open the top and *voilà*. They all fly away. Okay?"

"Um," I said.

Before I could say anything else, he popped the top of the box. A swarm of bees whirled out, heading toward

Wilder, who hopped back into the car and slammed the door. The black-and-yellow swirl crashed against the window, then rose upward.

"Release the smoke!" Pierre yelled.

"They're already going crazy!"

The current of bees turned toward me.

"Smoke!" Pierre yelled again.

I pressed down on the bag and shot out a cloud of smoke. This made the bees even angrier. They darted toward my gloves. I flinched and dropped the smoker. The buzzing intensified, as if the bees were cheering.

"Get the smoker!" Pierre called over the roaring buzz. "They will attack if you are being weak. You must be strong!"

"I'm . . . strong!" I yelped, flailing my wrists, swatting away bracelets of bees before picking up the smoker.

"Big smoke!" Pierre yelled. "Punch. Punch."

"What?" I screamed.

Pierre pretended to box.

I punched the bag, releasing a gigantic plume of smoke. The bees darted, taking shelter in the nearest tall tree. I punched the bag again.

"So long, bad boys!" Pierre called to the bees retreating through clouds of smoke. He continued to loudly curse them until they disappeared from view.

"And the good boy—how are you feeling?" he asked me once he regained his composure.

My heartbeat thumped in my ears. I looked at Wilder in the car, his face still struck with fear as a few stray bees banged against the window. I couldn't help but smile.

"I feel amazing," I said.

"*Magnifique*," Pierre said. "Welcome to France."

SEVEN

After ridding ourselves of the bad bees, it was time to collect the good bees. Pierre held a crumpled Post-it note with a rudimentary drawing of the woods and a large X marking the spot of a wild swarm. This was a one-person operation, he told me, and he leaped forward on his own, leaving me to wander back to the car.

When I opened the door, Wilder jumped and covered his exposed arms.

"Buzzzzzz," I said, sliding in beside him (still wearing the beekeeper suit).

"Not funny," he said. "I don't want to see a bee for the rest of the trip."

"I think that's one of the main things we'll be seeing. Bees generally like flowers and farms and stuff."

"Aren't bees supposed to be dying everywhere?" Wilder said.

"That's not a good thing."

"Sounds good to me."

"They seem to be thriving here," I said as Pierre ambled forward with a newly buzzing wooden box.

He popped the trunk and delicately pushed in the good bees, a few of which escaped into the back seat. Wilder grabbed the veiled helmet from my lap, dropped it over his head, and wrapped himself in a protective hug.

"How's it going, Wild Man?" Pierre asked after returning to the driver's seat.

"Fine," Wilder squeaked.

"These are the good ones, you know," Pierre tried to reassure him. "They will not be attacking you."

Wilder continued to look like a stormtrooper in the fetal position. "I'm good. Just not a big bee fan."

"It is no problem," Pierre said. "There is much else to do once we arrive." As the good bees circled Wilder's helmet, Pierre started the car and we sped out of the woods.

After twenty minutes I recognized the road Pierre had traveled in his introduction video. We passed several barns and stopped before the black iron gates of Château de Beaulieu.

"Ah, Michel," Pierre cooed. An older-looking teenager with long hair and loose overalls made his way to the entrance as slowly as possible.

"*Merci*," Pierre called out the window as the gates parted, revealing the majestic castle. The knowledge that its interior was crumbling and overrun by aggressive pigeons did not diminish its splendor. The gray bricks were polished, the red shutters washed, and the black-capped spires glinted in the sun. I tried to count the number of windows but lost track at nineteen.

"Not bad, eh?" Pierre said as he rolled the car to a stop. "Lunch should be ready soon."

"What about the bees?" I asked as Pierre left the car.

"They are fine."

"Our luggage?" Wilder asked.

"You can collect this later," Pierre said. "Follow me." He led us to the right of the castle, toward a small single-level house built from the same gray bricks.

We stepped over the landing and discovered that it wasn't a house, but a massive kitchen teeming with pots and pans. An eruption of French cursing met us as the two young cooks inside argued next to the oven.

"These are last summer's scoff-airs," Pierre said. "Having a little disagreement about the lunch menu."

The cooks immediately straightened at Pierre's words, gave us a little bow, and said, "*Bonjour.*"

"Lunch is . . . in . . . a . . . ten . . . min-ute," one said while the other congratulated him on his English.

"Bravo," Pierre said, agreeing. "You have become very good." He turned to us. "Now you can answer in French. You have done studying, yes?"

"Yes," Wilder said.

"Some," I said.

"Thank you for this wonderful meal," Wilder said swiftly in French. I knew he was lying about only practicing during our tutoring sessions. His mom always made him study on weekends during the school year.

Pierre and the cooks smiled approvingly and turned toward me.

"Thank you . . . for . . . a . . . dinner . . . nice," I stumbled out.

The cooks looked confused, but Pierre gave me an encouraging thumbs-up. He patted them on the back and pushed open a rickety screen door, revealing a long, white iron table set in the shade of an idyllic green yard. Around the table were thirteen chairs, nine of them filled with people calling out greetings in different languages. It was overwhelming to say the least.

"We can do the introductions later," Pierre said, taking his position at the very end of the table. The two remaining seats were next to (1) an impossibly good-looking girl in animated conversation with the impossibly good-looking boy next to her, and (2) a tall and frail boy cleaning his glasses with the bottom of his mustard-colored T-shirt.

Before I could even think of moving in the direction of the girl, Wilder was halfway around the table, turning on his "charm" and asking, in French, whether the seat next to her was taken.

I waved to the frail boy, who was still cleaning his glasses and did not give any indication that he had seen me.

"Hello," I said as I sat down.

He put his glasses back on, inspected my face, but said nothing.

"Should we do the face kisses?" I suggested.

"I am German." He extended his hand. "Martin."

"Rylan," I said, surprised by the firmness of his grip.

"American?" he asked.

"Yes. How did you know?"

"Your face. Your clothes. Your accent."

"Is that bad?"

"That is your decision."

"You're saying it in a negative way."

"I am only answering in response to your question."

"Would you be offended if I said, 'You are so German.'"

"I *am* German," he said.

"Never mind," I said. "So, what, uh, brought you here?"

"It is lunchtime."

"I mean originally. To the farm."

"I am here for SCOFF. Students Communing on French Farms."

"You're interested in farming?"

"Of course."

I looked around the table, where everyone else's conversations flowed across language barriers with ease. I could have tried to join the discussion to my right but felt bad leaving Martin to stare into his empty plate in silence. (Though that did seem to be his preference.)

"When did you get here?" I asked him.

"I arrived this morning by train," Martin said.

"From Germany?"

He looked at me coldly. "Why so much questioning?"

"I'm just trying to make conversation," I said.

"American conversation."

"We can have a German conversation if you want."

"You speak German?" he asked.

"*Nein*," I said, enunciating the only German word I knew.

I was expecting at least a little smile but got a look empty of all emotion. "Then we cannot have a German conversation."

"You said you were here to commune," I said.

"Are we not communing?"

"I'm trying to, but . . ."

"You have *communed* with me for five minutes, and what have you learned?"

"That you're German."

"Exact. And do you know what *I* have learned by sitting in quiet for twenty minutes?"

I shook my head. Martin leaned toward me and, in hushed tones, described what he had gathered about the other six SCOFFers. In conversation with Wilder were three French students fresh from their first year at École fantastique d'horticulture. As its name suggests, it is one of the best gardening schools in the country, though only one of them—Michel—was actually interested in horticulture. The other two—Emile and Simone—were enrolled at the school and this summer program by their parents. Emile's father had founded the most successful eco-friendly bottled water company in northern France and wanted his son to be connected to the natural world. And Simone—

"That's like Wilder's mom!" I interrupted.

"This is what they have been discussing," Martin said. "Your friend's mother made some kind of water-drinking phone application?"

"An app that reminds people to drink water," I said.

"Americans cannot remember to drink water?"

"You get points, too, if you drink eight glasses a day."

"What do the points do?"

"You just get them."

"You cannot buy something with these points?"

"No, you just have them. Well, if you have enough points at the end of the week, you get, like, a picture of a cup with a star on it."

"This is a popular application?"

"Very."

Martin took a long sip from his water glass. "One point."

"Look at you, making a joke," I said.

A surprisingly loud squawk of a laugh erupted from Martin, startling the rest of the table.

"*It wasn't* that *funny*," I whispered.

I asked him about the other two students. Annie, from Hong Kong, was an artist of some kind. She spoke deliberately with a slightly British tinge, and her voice often dipped out of earshot. But Martin had gathered that she was planning to move to Canada for high school and wanted to practice her French language skills. She was talking to a tiny ten-year-old Swiss girl named Lia, who spoke animatedly and precisely and was easy to hear over everyone else. At a table of mostly teenagers, she looked the most out of place.

"And what brought her here?" I asked Martin.

"She loves nature."

"Don't we all," I said.

"I do not," Martin said. "But I respect it."

The kitchen doors swung open and conversations stopped as everyone marveled at the feast headed toward the table. There was grilled fish, roasted potatoes, three different salads, six loaves of bread, a slab of butter the size of a dictionary, and plate after plate of aromatic cheeses.

"*Bon appétit*," Pierre said, and motioned for us to begin.

EIGHT

As we settled into a dessert of even more bread (but sweet this time), Pierre rose from his chair.

"I hope you have all enjoyed your meal." He paused to light a cigarette. As the smoke wafted over the table, he continued. "It is the custom now to take a short rest, but you cannot do this without a place to sleep, no?"

"I can sleep on the ground," Martin said.

"Beneath a tree," Lia offered.

The French kids laughed.

"You *can* do these things," Pierre said, "but there are beds as well, and we must decide who will be sleeping where."

"How do we decide?" I asked.

Pierre's eyes sparkled. "*We* do not. We leave it to *the fates.*" He swirled his hand in the air, leaving a curlicue of smoke.

"*Which* fates?" Wilder asked.

"I need you all to find a leaf," Pierre said.

Everyone except Lia stared at him in confusion. She produced a leaf from her pocket.

"Go," Pierre declared. "You have one minute."

I stumbled out of my chair and went toward the nearest tree trunk, trying to find the best leaf, though unsure of what made any particular leaf the best. Everyone else seemed equally vexed but rushed to decide once Pierre started counting down from five.

"Follow me. And bring your leaf, of course," he said, leading us toward a wide-open field.

I sidled next to Wilder and Simone.

"Did you get a good leaf?" I asked Wilder.

"This guy is nuts," Wilder said.

"What does this mean, *nuts?*" Simone asked.

Wilder and I started laughing.

"It is a funny word?" Simone persisted.

"It has different meanings," Wilder said. "In this case it means that Pierre is bananas."

Simone was even more confused.

"He is not *all there* in his head," Wilder clarified.

"No, I do not think what you say is true," Simone said. "I think that he is being fun. Look at my leaf." She spun her leaf in front of Wilder's eyes.

Wilder giggled. Not laughed but *giggled*.

"I guess you're right." He spun his leaf in front of her face. "He is *being fun*."

Simone playfully knocked his hand out of her face.

"Anyone want to see my leaf?" I said. But they weren't listening.

In the center of the field, Pierre asked us to form a line. There were two living quarters, he explained. While he *could* divide us up into boys and girls or try to mix everyone up, this was not how he liked to do things. He preferred to let the spiritual world guide him.

We were to take turns standing still, holding our leaf overhead, and then let it go. By the movement of the fates, the leaves would organize themselves into two distinct groups.

"Let me demonstrate," Pierre said. He raised his green leaf in the air and let go. It sailed on the wind to his left, fluttered, and landed softly on the ground.

"Where would you stay?" Martin asked.

"I have my own room," Pierre said. "But you see how it works?"

Everyone mumbled some version of agreement, except Martin, who said no.

"Then let us begin. Lia . . ." She skipped over, raised her verdant leaf, and let go. The wind lifted the leaf a few inches before it spun to the ground. Lia bowed and skipped back.

The process continued as, one by one, everyone released their leaves to the fates. The fates must not have felt that passionately about our sleeping arrangements, as the leaves fell into more of a single pile than two distinct clumps. Nevertheless, there were certain leaves that didn't touch others, and that was enough for the groups to start forming.

So far, the fates had organized the French students— Michel and Emile—into one group, and the international students—Annie, Lia, and Martin—into another. Wilder and I waited at the end of the line while Simone released her leaf. As it drifted through the air, Michel and Emile cheered for her leaf to touch theirs, which, of course, it did.

Wilder was up next. He let his leaf tumble into the fates, and cheers exploded from the French contingent as it landed on the edge of Michel's. Despite only knowing him for an hour, they were already singing "Wild Thing" as Wilder pumped his fist and accepted their enthusiastic group hug.

"Do I even need to go?" I asked Pierre.

"Of course. It is possible the fates believe we must have

one group of five and one group of three."

"Really?" I beamed.

To my surprise, Wilder led the French students in a chant of "*Ry-lan! Ry-lan! Ry-lan!*" The other group stood with their hands in their pockets. I raised my lightly torn leaf, closed my eyes, and let go.

The leaf floated over to the two piles, careened one way, then another. It looked ready to land on Wilder's leaf when a last gust of the fates pushed it to fall on top of Martin's.

Pierre clasped his hands together. "The *fates* believe in *symmetry*."

I looked over at Wilder. He mouthed "Sorry," but didn't look too disappointed. I sighed and joined the group the fates had picked for me.

Martin extended his hand. "Welcome aboard."

NINE

After guiding Wilder and the French students to their small cottage, Pierre led our group behind the castle, through the woods, past a field of long grass, and toward a sizable horse stable.

"You have horses?!" Lia squealed as we stepped through a doorway with no door.

"In the past," Pierre said. "But I have let these horses free."

"You just set them free?" I said.

"Yes, take down the door, and away they go. So now there is space for you."

"But we're not horses," I said.

"Which is the reason for the beds." Pierre pointed to

four cots stacked in the corner. "I will let you decide who will take which area."

"You mean which horse stall," I said.

Pierre smiled. "A feisty one. You would make a good horse."

"I don't want to be a horse. Why can't we stay in a real house like the other group?" Although I could handle bees, I was having trouble picturing myself in such uncomfortable living quarters for the next month.

"It is nice out here," Pierre said. "There is more nature."

"I love it," Lia said, leaping into a bundle of hay and taking a deep, satisfied sniff.

Martin surveyed the cots as if he were an expert in cot construction. "These will certainly do." He popped the legs out and ran his hands over them. "Very sturdy."

I looked to Annie, who seemed equally disappointed to spend the next month as a horse. She shrugged. "It is . . . adequate."

"*Parfait*," Pierre said, making his way to the exit. "You can do whatever you would like for the rest of the day. Dinner is at nine o'clock."

"Nine o'clock?!" I gasped.

Pierre gave a knowing look to the others and said, "American."

They all laughed as Pierre slid out and whistled away.

"Why is it so funny that I'm American?" I asked.

"It just is," Martin said, carrying a cot over for me. "Americans are funny. Look at you, being irritated." He set down my cot and scrunched up his face in an impression of an irritated American. "'I will not sleep in the barn! I deserve a mansion!'"

"It's unreasonable to expect a room and a bed?" I asked.

"It is not unreasonable. He placed his cot directly next to mine and lay down. "But this is not too bad."

Lia rolled out of the hay and dragged her cot over. "We could push all of our beds together and make a super-bed."

"I like a little space." Martin moved his cot a few inches from Lia's. "But I appreciate the idea."

Lia didn't seem offended. She was testing out the strength of her cot by lightly bouncing up and down.

"Aren't you disappointed that you won't be able to practice your French?" I asked Annie, who was sitting on a pile of hay, looking out the window.

"What?" she said absentmindedly.

"Aren't you here to learn French? To commune with French students?" I asked.

"To commune on French farms," Martin corrected.

"How do you know that?" Annie said.

I pointed to Martin. "He was eavesdropping at lunch."

"That's not very nice," Annie said.

"What is *eavesdropping*?" Lia asked.

Martin said, "It is being observant."

Annie said, "It is being rude."

I said, "Do you want the official definition?"

"Please," Lia said.

"It's like when, um—" I started.

"This does not sound official," Martin interjected.

"It's when you are secretly listening to a private conversation," I said.

"Oh, that does sound rude," Lia said.

"In Germany, being a good listener is considered a valuable skill," Martin said.

"When someone is speaking with you," Annie said.

"In all circumstances," Martin said.

"He *is* very good at listening," I said. "He told me about you, too." I pointed to Lia. "How you love nature and—"

"Insects," Lia finished my sentence.

"Ah," Martin said. "I thought you were saying *incense*. Insects is much more sensible."

"And who are you?" Annie asked Martin. "You know so much about us."

Martin sat up. "I am Martin, fourteen, from Germany. I intend to become a farmer. My purpose here is to learn more about organic farming and improve my French vocabularies."

He extended his hand back toward Annie.

"I am Annie, also fourteen, from Hong Kong, as you know. Soon I will move to Canada, as you know. And . . . what is it that you don't know?"

"You are some kind of artist?" Martin said.

"Yes. I am also a dedicated artist," Annie answered.

"How so?" I asked.

"I make art every day," Annie said. "Mostly drawing when I was younger, but now I am largely in a period of painting. But also photography and some digital design."

Everyone's eyes turned toward me.

"I'm Rylan. Twelve, soon to be thirteen, from—I mean, you know already." I looked around and tried to decide how to continue. "I'm here because, well, my friend Wilder invited me and we are, or were, best friends, and I guess I hoped that . . ." I trailed off as I envisioned Wilder going through the same impromptu orientation in the cottage. He wouldn't say that he was here to save our friendship. He was here to have fun, to meet girls, and to compare lifestyle tips with the rich French students.

"Hoped that . . ." Annie prodded.

"Hoped that maybe I could make some new friends, too," I said.

Annie and Lia smiled.

"American," Martin murmured from his cot, his eyes closed.

"Are you sleeping already?" I asked.

"It has been a busy morning," Martin mumbled.

I turned back to Annie. "You never answered the question."

"Which question?"

"If you are disappointed with our—" I gestured to the bales of hay.

Annie sighed. "Well, yes, I am feeling a little bit of disappointment. But I do like the light in here." Her gaze followed a patch of sunlight on the stable floor. "And all the open space. As long as *someone* won't be listening to all of my conversations, it will be a suitable arrangement."

Martin smiled from his reclined position. "I cannot turn off my ears, but I can be more respectful. Good night."

Annie and Lia stretched out onto their cots.

"Good night," Lia said.

I lay down on my cot, closed my eyes, and, to my surprise, quickly fell asleep.

TEN

I woke with a shiver. Martin remained sleeping next to me, but the stable was otherwise empty. I got up and stumbled outside, rubbing my hands across my bare arms and wishing I had a sweatshirt. I turned back to the stable but remembered that all my things were still in the back seat of Pierre's car. Had it really been only a few hours?

I hadn't emailed Mom or Serena yet, let alone thought about if, when, and how I would send a message to my father. So I wandered through the woods with my phone, trying to catch a Wi-Fi signal. There were still no bars, but I did hear quickly approaching footsteps behind me. Fearing some sort of stampede, I pressed my back into a tree and crouched down low.

I held my breath as Annie and Lia ran past.

"Hey!" I yelled.

They both jumped, the surprise reversed.

Annie turned. "Are you . . . hiding?"

"No," I said. "I was just coming to look for you."

"By crouching behind a tree?" Annie said.

"It's an American thing. You wouldn't understand." I brushed off the back of my shirt. "Why are you running, anyway?"

"She challenged me to a race," Annie said.

"Which I was winning," Lia said. "I am the fastest in my grade."

"I am one of the slowest," Annie said.

"It looked competitive," I said.

"Her legs are longer," Lia said, who was, at best, four feet, five inches tall. Annie was four years older and at least eight inches taller. "And I was on purpose slowing myself down to not cause her embarrassment."

"You are such a liar," Annie said, playfully pushing Lia.

Lia pushed her back, then asked me, "Are *you* fast?"

"I'm normal. Average."

It was easy to see that Lia was bursting to race again.

"Probably faster than you, though," I teased.

Lia clapped her hands. "First one back to the barn."

"Why back to the barn?" I asked.

"To wake Martin for dinner," Lia said.

"The first person to wake Martin is the winner," I agreed.

"I can be the referee," Annie said. "One race is enough for me."

Annie drew a line in the moist soil with her shoe, and Lia and I lined up behind it. Annie counted down from three, and Lia took off like a rabbit. I kept pace until we left the woods, and then she rocketed ahead.

When I caught up to her in the barn, Martin was sitting straight up with a puzzled look on his face.

"You lost!" Lia cried before collapsing on her cot.

Dinner proceeded like lunch: course upon course of food brought from the kitchen by last summer's SCOFFers. It began with loaves of bread and slabs of sea-salted butter, followed by a cold soup with fresh tomatoes and olive oil. Nearly full at this point, I barely had any of the pâté, which smelled like hummus made from meat, and I avoided the plate of pork rillette, which looked like churned cat food. After one slice of tender steak I was entirely full, but that didn't stop me from eating the chocolate mousse and final plates of cheese. By this time, the sky had turned from pink to black. Pierre brought out two candles and positioned them between the dirtied dishes. Using the tip of his burning cigarette, he lit both.

Then he returned to his seat and called for a moment of silence. He closed his eyes, inhaled deeply, his breath lifting his posture upward, and then breathed out, allowing his body to crumple forward. With a flourish, he popped his head back up and exclaimed, "It has been a beautiful day, and I am so pleased to have you all here. The real work will begin tomorrow, but for tonight, we have one final tradition." He slipped his hand into his pocket and lifted out a pack of worn cards with elaborate symbols.

"These cards," Pierre said, spreading the deck before him, "are *le Tarot de Marseille*. They are in my family for many years and have been the guide for many decisions. Before I do anything new, I always ask the Tarot how it will be. It is my tradition to offer each of you a reading tonight if you have questions about how the next month will be for you."

"How does it work?" I asked.

"Ah, the first volunteer," Pierre said.

"I was more just wondering, like, what it involved," I said.

"It is better if I show you," Pierre said.

My face reddened as all eyes turned toward me. "In front of *everyone*?" I asked.

"If it is okay with the rest," Pierre said.

Everyone at the table encouraged me. I looked at Wilder, and he smiled back at me. "Okay," I agreed. "What do I do?"

"*Très bien*," Pierre said. "You must only think of a question."

I already knew the question I wanted to ask. "And then what?"

"And then the Tarot will tell you the answer. Understand?"

"Not exactly," I said.

"It is okay," Pierre said. "Just . . . *think*." He tapped the center of his forehead three times. "Are you holding the question?"

In my mind I slowly enunciated my question: *Should I meet my father?*

"Keep holding the question in your mind," Pierre said as he cut the deck. "Now." He leaned forward, the contours of his face lit by candlelight. "*Send it* to me."

I stared into his eyes and repeated the question in my head.

Pierre raised his eyebrows and moved his face out of the flame. He placed his hands on the half deck to his right and selected the top three cards. Carefully, he flipped each card over, emitting a small gasp with each reveal.

"What is it?" I asked, straining to see them. "Is it bad?"

"There is no bad, or good," Pierre said. "Only truth. What. Will. Be." He paused to let this sit with the rest of the table. Then he leaned forward to narrate my future.

He placed his index finger on the first overturned card. "This is you now, the . . . uh . . . I don't know the English. *Valet d'Epée.* You see it is a young man with a sword, which means he has some strength, he can be strong, and have passion, but his face, it is looking down. No smile, staring at the dirt. This could mean many things. But it is especially in-ter-es-ting because you see at the other end is *le Roi de Bâton*, the King of Wands, and he is also looking away. Not back at you, the young man. And in between these two is the Four of Cups, a very *important* card." Pierre stopped to smile at me knowingly.

"Important how?" I asked.

"Important because the Four of Cups means a journey. You no longer have satisfaction with how things are. You need to change. Get a new"—he tapped the table— "foundation. Yes? I see in your face this is correct."

I didn't know what my face was doing, but he was correct.

"So," Pierre said, pointing toward the young man with the sword, "if this is you today, looking down, uncertain but with strength." He traced his index finger across the table to the king. "And this is you at the end of the month—a king, with power, looking toward the future." His finger looped back to the center card. "Then you must make a change. And let these two"—he lifted up the young man and the king—"face each other."

He held the two cards next to each other as the rest of the table clapped.

My heart was beating rapidly. I knew what I had to do.

"Who's next?" Pierre asked, wiping my future back into a stack of cards.

ELEVEN

As Pierre divined the futures of the others at the table, I pretended to have a restroom emergency and snuck off to his small stone cottage. During dinner he said this was the only place on the property with a reliable Wi-Fi connection. The mess inside surprised me. Clothes covered the floor, hay was strewn about randomly, and the only visible chair was precariously stacked with books. I perched on the edge of Pierre's unmade bed, took out my phone, and started to type.

"H—"

What was the right greeting: *Hi Dad? Hello Father? Hey Mr. O'Hare?*

I wanted to show my interest in meeting him, but not come off as desperate. I didn't *need* to meet him. I just happened to be in France, and heard that he was too, so why shouldn't we maybe meet up. Just to get to know each other.

"Hello," I typed.

At school, the teachers taught us how to "properly" write emails. It was best, they said, to start with a warm greeting and a compliment before you said what you actually wanted. I always found this difficult but tried my best.

This is ~~your son~~ Rylan and ~~mom said~~ I heard that you just got married. ~~and wanted to make up for some of the mistakes that~~ Congratulations! ~~It must be nice to find someone new who you want to~~ I also heard that you live in Paris now. I know it's been a long time since we saw each other, but I'm also in France for the summer for a kind of vacation thing. If you wanted to meet up in Paris, I will be there on July 15. ~~It would mean a lot to me to see you if you~~ If you aren't busy, please let me know and I can meet pretty much anywhere in the city. ~~Mom's friend, Serena,~~ A friend of mine is helping me use the trains and I'm never late.

The teachers also taught us to not be too forceful in our email closing. To keep things friendly and light.

I ~~really~~ hope to hear from you soon.

~~Love,~~

Rylan

I reviewed my edited email a few times, reading it out loud and trying to imagine my dad reading it at 10:30 p.m. Maybe it would be better to wait until the morning?

"Halloo!" rang from the door.

I jumped, pressing my palm into the front of my phone. A *whoosh* filled the air as Martin rushed into Pierre's room.

"Are you finished with the toilet?" he asked, shifting from foot to foot.

"The what?" I said, looking from my phone to him with what must have been a pained expression.

"The—are you okay?" Martin asked.

"I'm fine," I said. "Just homesick is all." I held up my phone. "Sending a, uh, message. An email."

Martin squirmed. "I need quite badly to use the washroom. But if you are sick for your home and want to talk about this, we can do this in a minute." He scurried to the bathroom and slammed the door.

I went through my sent messages to confirm the *whoosh*. It had indeed gone through and was now a blue dot in his inbox, waiting to be clicked. I kept staring at my phone for thirty seconds, a minute. Just to see if, maybe, he was also staring at his phone at that very moment. And would quickly write me back.

I didn't *feel* like a knight thrusting his sword forward, but I had done my part. Now it was up to the king to look backward or keep staring straight ahead.

TWELVE

The next morning, I woke to the smell of hay. It took a minute to remember where I was. And then another minute to remember the message I'd sent the night before and to scramble off my cot.

When I made it to the bench outside Pierre's cottage, I pulled up my email and swiped down. I stared at the whirling wheel, hoping it would deliver.

Finally, it did. There were two new messages: one from Serena and a summer homework reminder from school. Nothing from Michael O'Hare.

I looked at the time: 7:53 a.m. That was pretty early, I guess. Especially for the summer. Maybe he was making coffee. Maybe he waited until after his first sip to check his email. Mom never responded to emails before having at least two cups of coffee.

As I contemplated my father's morning routine, the window in front of me popped open.

"I heard footsteps" came Pierre's voice. "Is there an early riser?"

"It's me. Rylan." I moved to the window to show my face. "Sorry for waking you up."

"Wake *me*!" Pierre said. He was sitting at a table next to the window with a newspaper and a stack of books. "No, no, no. I have been awake for two hours at minimum." He lifted his reading stack. "Adding nutrients for the mind. *Typically*, the students do not start the day until eleven or so, so . . ."

"So I should go back to sleep?"

"Or nourish your mind." He smiled, tossing me a copy of a French newspaper titled *Le Monde*. "Practice your French."

He gathered his books and joined me outside. "Coffee or tea for you?"

"What are you having?" I asked.

"Always coffee."

"Coffee for me, then."

"You go out and start reading," he said, waving to the table where we had eaten dinner. "*Café* will be *on* the *way*."

I took a seat in the middle of the massive table and unfolded *Le Monde*, deciphering as many words as I could on the first two pages.

Pierre came out with a fluffy croissant and a large mug filled to the brim.

"Enjoying the world?" he asked.

"Parts of it," I said between the three bites it took to eat the entire croissant. "People's names and the numbers."

"Slow *doowwnn*," Pierre prompted as I moved from the croissant to the coffee.

"I'm sorry," I said. "I'm just really hungry for some reason."

"The reason is the change in time," Pierre said. "But still, you must *relax*. Like this." He leaned back, took a deep breath in, then out. "It is morning. Smell the trees, the grass, the ink of the newspaper. There is no rush."

I sat back in the chair and inhaled, picking up the rich aroma of the coffee, the lingering scent of Pierre's half-eaten pastry, the cool morning air.

"That is much better, no?" Pierre said.

I nodded, raised the mug, and took a sip. My face scrunched at the taste, hotter and more bitter than I had expected.

Pierre laughed. "I make it strong. Be careful."

"Won't this speed me back up?" I asked.

"Your mind, yes, and your heartbeat. But if you focus on reading and being relaxed, it will help you to be . . ." He collapsed into the back of his chair in a state of total relaxation.

Then he quickly popped up. "But for me it is time to bring the good bees from the car."

I leaned back, sipped coffee, looked through pictures of French politicians, and settled into the rhythm of the morning.

When I heard Wilder's voice, I set aside *Le Monde* to listen. He was being encouraged to mock American breakfast foods, which I knew he loved. The French students repeated "Leggo my Eggo" and devolved into laughter.

As they approached the table, Wilder made eye contact and raised his eyebrows in my direction, but instead of taking the chair next to me, he sat at the end of the table. Michel, Simone, and Emile filled in around him, leaving an empty seat between me and their group.

"*Bonjour*," I tried to say brightly.

The French students responded with another eruption of laughter.

A look of dismay crossed Wilder's face before he joined them.

I looked down, unsure of what I'd done wrong but deeply embarrassed nonetheless.

"We are sorry," Simone said when she'd caught her breath. "It is a little joke between us. How Americans say *bonjoouurrrr*."

My face grew hot, the caffeine accelerating my natural reactions. "I can see how that's funny. I'll, uh, try to say it differently next time." I forced a polite smile.

"No, no," Simone continued. "It is okay. It is only that I, we, can get a little silly in the morning." She tried to straighten herself out. "How is your, ah, stay, your evening in the . . ."

"Stables," I filled in.

"*Stables?*" Wilder repeated.

"Former stables," I said. "There are some cots now. Mixed in with the hay. But it's not too bad. How about your—"

"Cottage," Wilder filled in. "It's okay. A little messier than I was expecting. But no hay."

"And one spider *spéciale*," Simone said jokingly.

They all looked at Michel, who playfully responded in French with something about never killing spiders.

"You've become pretty close in one day," I said.

"We have been friends already," Simone said, circling her hand toward the other French students. "And it has been easy to add your *best friend*, Wilder."

They all started cracking up again.

Wilder looked down, but a smile escaped his lips.

"I think I'm missing this joke," I said.

"It's nothing," Wilder said. "An inside joke."

"I like jokes," Lia said as she walked up with Annie and Martin.

"It's not that kind of joke," Wilder said.

"I know a Swiss joke if you want to hear," Lia said.

Wilder assented.

"What did the Swiss mountaineer say when she came to a mountain where global warming was starting to reverse itself?"

She paused to survey her audience, most of whom seemed confused by the wordy setup, then said, "Let's go climate!"

Martin squawked out a laugh, and I joined in.

"There is a good joke about the Swiss that they say in Germany," Martin said. "How do you make a Swiss roll?"

"How?" Lia asked.

"Push them off the Alps."

Everyone laughed, but Lia shook her head. "This one is not nice. A Swiss would not push someone down a mountain."

"A German would," Wilder said, to the delight of the French students.

Martin smiled. "I know an American joke."

"Go on," Wilder urged.

"What is the difference between the US and a yogurt?" He paused. "If you leave a yogurt alone for three hundred years, it will develop a culture."

"I see the two camps are getting along," said Pierre from the door of the kitchen. He had changed into paint-stained overalls and held a wide-brimmed hat.

"We are behaving contentiously," Lia said matter-of-factly.

"Nevertheless," Pierre said, "it is time to begin our work." Without waiting for anyone to get up, he began strolling in the direction of the gardens, whistling a jaunty tune.

THIRTEEN

There were two gardens of equal size next to each other, separated by thirty feet of untamed grass. One garden was already thriving. While Pierre led us through, he pointed out the vegetables—artichokes, leeks, lettuce, chard, and tomatoes—and explained how the garden was the success of last year's program. He had replanted the same vegetables a few weeks earlier, and with careful attention to weeding and watering and pruning, the garden would be successful again.

The second garden was *not* thriving; in fact, it could barely be called a garden. It was mostly a collection of tall grass and weeds, maybe a tomato or two, clumps of hay, and some garbage cans tipped on their sides.

Its appearance, Pierre explained, was the result of its journey toward becoming a certifiably organic garden. He'd had to let it sit idle for the past three years, not using any artificial fertilizers or pesticides, so that the soil could return to its original state. The process now complete, it was ready to be transformed into something that grew more than weeds.

The goal was to have ripe vegetables from both gardens ready to sell at the annual Dreux Summer Festival on July 13, the last Saturday we would spend on the farm. Pierre had operated a booth there since revitalizing his uncle's property, and the previous summer had been the most successful ever. This year, with both gardens fully operational, he hoped to have even more customers and raise his standing in the local farming community.

"I asked my neighbor, a master farmer, for a bit of advice. And he agreed to put some good things in for us," Pierre explained as he walked us through the tangled garbage patch. "If you look under the grass, you can see the zucchini, tomato, asparagus, and this is the start of the lettuce."

"But your neighbor left all this grass?" I asked.

"He is not a lawn mower," Pierre said. "However, he did recommend that we remove it. Along with some other suggestions." He reached into the front pocket of his overalls and removed a torn piece of graph paper. "Rip away the weeds, make some compost, pay attention to the soil, supply water each day, avoid all pests, and grow the vegetables well. Okay? You can start."

Martin raised his hand.

"You can just speak," Pierre said.

"Do you have an instruction for how we should start?" Martin asked.

"No, not really," Pierre said. "You should do whatever it is that calls to you. Is of interest to you."

Martin instinctively raised his hand again but quickly lowered it.

"It would perhaps be better if we created a plan," he suggested.

"*Better* I am not sure," Pierre responded. "It would be *different*."

"Possibly it would be more helpful," Martin said. "If, for example, we divide the two gardens. This is a German practice. I don't know the translation. We call it *schrebergarten*. There are large public gardens in my city, and families can apply to take care of a personal patch."

"You are all feeling like a family already, eh?" Pierre grinned, circling his fingers around Martin, Annie, Lia, and me.

"Somewhat," Martin said, a little confused. "But more my suggestion is about how we can best organize our labor."

"I like this idea!" Emile called. "Our family will take the other garden."

Simone, Michel, and Wilder all laughed.

"Well, it is not exactly as I had *envisioned*," Pierre said. "But if everyone would like to do two family gardens, then—"

Emile raised his fist in the air and hollered, "*Schwebergarden!*"

"*Schrebergarten,*" Martin corrected. "And yes, we accept this garden."

Wilder and the French students continued laughing as they walked off to their garden, echoes of their mocking German impressions still audible.

I poked through the dense grass with my foot, trying to find a vegetable. I glared at Martin. "Why would you pick *this*?"

"The purpose of a *schrebergarten* is to learn new things," Martin said.

"We could learn new things with *that* garden," I said, pointing to the actual garden.

"I already know how to water vegetables," Martin said. "What I have not done is to build an organic garden out of garbage and weeds."

"Do you know how?" I asked.

"Not yet, but I have some ideas."

I stared at him.

"To begin, I am going to plan a trench between the vegetable rows. You could be my partner in this planning . . ."

"Um," I said. "I feel like we should probably start with all the grass and weeds."

"Certainly, that is also important," Martin said, only slightly disappointed. "However, I still plan to go to the internet bench to prepare my research, if you want to join me later."

He walked off, and I pushed my way through the tall grass, trying to find where Lia and Annie had disappeared to.

Lia was on her knees, inspecting a ladybug as it nibbled a stalk of grass. Annie was lying on her back, with her phone pointed toward the sky.

"You get service here?" I asked.

"I am using my phone as a tool. A camera," Annie said.

"Taking grass selfies?"

"Pictures of the sky. But that's a good idea." She pressed her phone's reverse-orientation button, held up a peace sign, and took a grass selfie.

"*You should take a picture of this,*" Lia whispered. "*The thirteen-spotted lady beetle.*"

"Wooowwww," Annie marveled, zooming in to capture each spot.

She passed me her phone so I could also marvel.

"Wow," I said, unmarveled, because I was starting to worry that I'd have to pull out all the grass by myself as the rest of my "family" did research, took pictures, and inspected for unique insects.

"I have never seen one with so many spots," Annie said.

"It is what makes them special," Lia said. "Most common is the seven-spotted, but there is also the nine-spotted, the ten-spotted—"

"The eleven-spotted," I continued, sensing a trend.

"In fact, no," Lia said. "An eleven-spotted lady beetle has never been seen. But there is the twelve-spotted, thirteen-spotted, eighteen—"

"I think we get it," I said.

Lia looked slightly hurt.

"I'm sorry," I said. "You can finish."

"And the twenty-two-spotted," Lia finished. "Can you imagine!"

"That *is* a lot of spots," I said. "But we should maybe start working a little or—"

"If we waited several months, the lady beetles would take care of the grass," Lia said. "We wouldn't have to pull anything."

"But since we only have *one* month, we could maybe start removing the grass ourselves?" I suggested. "The patches the lady beetles aren't eating."

I curled my fingers around a handful of grass, ready to pull it up by the roots.

"Wait!" Lia squealed. "I want to inspect it first!"

She leaned over and quickly scanned the bunch gathered in my hand. "It is safe," she said, relieved.

I ripped out the grass, walked to one of the tipped-over trash cans, and threw in the remains. As I dragged the trash can closer to the edge of our garden patch, Lia said, "This spot is also clear."

"Are you going to help me pull?" I asked.

"I am better at inspecting for insect harm," she said. "You are good at pulling the grass."

"How about Annie?" I asked.

She was still lying on her back and now seemed to be asleep. I gently called her name a few times, but she didn't respond.

"*Change in time,*" Lia whispered.

"The time changed for me too, you know," I said.

Lia pointed to a new square of tall grass. "This patch is clear."

As Annie snoozed in the sun and Martin worked on his trench construction plan, I got down on my knees and plucked one carefully inspected handful of grass at a time. It was slow at first, but Lia eventually joined me, and we made good progress through one row of our *schrebergarten*.

FOURTEEN

By eight o'clock, I was sweaty, exhausted, and, as promised, "fragrant with dirt," but the day's tasks were not yet done. As with the gardens, we had decided to split the dinner responsibilities rather than cooking as a large group. Unfortunately, the fates had decided that my group would cook the first meal.

While Pierre, the French students, and Wilder washed up and relaxed, we had an hour to prepare a dinner large and satisfying enough for nine people. The full contents of the kitchen—an overflowing refrigerator, fully stocked pantry, and a table lined with vegetables fresh from neighboring gardens—were available to us, but our limited cooking experience made it more overwhelming than exciting.

I had cooked before, but never for more than two people or beyond the instructions on the back of a pasta box. What I mean is: I'd made spaghetti and sometimes pressed Start on the microwave. I could also put chicken nuggets into the oven, but not always successfully.

Adding to our difficulty in deciding on a main dish was the fact that Martin and Lia were both vegetarian. That ruled out the chicken, duck, and goose. Instead, Martin suggested lentils.

"*Just* lentils?" I said.

"They have many nutrients," Martin said while scanning the kitchen for side dishes. "We can also have . . . the bread and . . . butter."

"This is too bland," Annie said. "A dinner plate should be colorful. My grandmother always says this."

"We could include a colorful vegetable," Martin said.

"I could make a salad!" Lia enthused. "I have seen my papa make it many times."

"And I could prepare the dressing," Annie said.

"The dressing?" Lia wondered.

"The . . . sauce for the salad," Annie answered.

"And I could pick out some cheese for dessert," I offered.

Martin rubbed his hands together in excitement before poorly attacking a bag of lentils with a knife.

Drawing on my extensive research, I selected three cheeses with distinctive flavors: a soft cheese, Camembert; a hard cheese, Comté; and a wrapped package marked *Goat* that smelled intriguing.

Martin stirred the boiling lentils to the beat of an aggressive techno song that blared from his ancient-looking iPod. Since he seemed so enraptured beating up the lentils, I joined Lia and Annie in slicing up vegetables.

They had different opinions about what should go into a salad and had compromised by adding every vegetable available.

"What do you normally put in your salad dressing?" Annie asked me.

"I don't know. Vinegar and little seeds and, you know, other stuff."

"Helpful," Annie said.

"I've only had the store-bought kind," I confessed.

"How does this sound?" She pronounced each ingredient as she tossed it into a silver bowl. "Vinegar. Salt. Pepper. Oil. Honey. Chili flakes." She tried to tap the bottom of the chili flake jar, but nothing came out. She tapped harder and harder until a flood of chili spilled out.

"It is good with some heat," she said.

"You did that on purpose?" I asked.

"It was not technically on purpose, but I am open to the possibility of a happy accident." She stirred the mostly red salad dressing. "It still needs something. A bit of interest. Maybe a spoon of mustard?"

"I'm not trying to criticize, but it looks a little *gross?*" I said.

"This is why I'm adding the mustard." She stirred a heaping glob of mustard into the mix and then lifted a spoon for me to test the flavor.

I tentatively licked the spoon. At first it was only mildly disgusting. But as the individual flavors bloomed across my taste buds, a wave of nausea sloshed through my stomach and exploded into an uncontrollable coughing fit.

"Water," I squeaked.

Lia rushed to fill a water glass while Annie sampled her own concoction.

"A little spicy," she agreed. "Maybe some more honey?"

I gave a thumbs-up while chugging water, but I didn't think honey could save it.

After adding more honey and remixing to her satisfaction, Annie poured the dressing over the salad and massaged it over each vegetable with her fingertips.

We took our dishes out to the others, who were lounging around the table.

"Tonight's menu: lentils," Martin announced, setting the pot of beans in the center of the table.

The French students looked confused, disappointed, and vaguely insulted.

"In addition, we have a fresh salad of lettuce, cucumber, tomato, leek, onion, pepper, radish, spinach, an assortment of nuts, and sauce," Lia said scientifically.

"With bread and cheese," I added, setting down my contribution.

Pierre smiled weakly and said, "*Bon appétit.*"

They did the opposite of digging in, hesitantly scooping lentils onto their plates.

"Very bean-y," Wilder said after his first bite.

"Thank you," Martin said between heaping spoonfuls.

"It wasn't a compliment," Wilder said.

"It is a *little* bland," Pierre said. "Did you see where I keep the spices?"

"Of course," Martin said. "But I prefer the natural flavor."

"I see," Pierre said, moving on to the salad. He took one bite and then spat it onto the ground as if it were a hair ball. "There . . . is . . . the . . . spice," he croaked, reaching for the bread and stuffing it into his mouth like a pacifier.

"Much better," he said after the bread absorbed the taste of the dressing. "I will keep to the bread and cheese."

I didn't think the lentils were that bad, but I also stayed away from the salad. Even Annie, despite her best efforts, couldn't eat more than a few bites.

As we ate, the evening gave way to night. At the end of the table, Pierre's cigarette glowed like a firefly. "I trust you have learned many new things today," he said. "But I am always looking for how we can make a better tomorrow. Does anyone have an idea?"

Calls for "more food," "better dinner," and "new chefs" sounded from the dark.

"We will see how the other group does tomorrow night," Pierre said, smiling toward Wilder and the French students. "But I agree. For our foreign visitors, I could provide some small cooking lessons. Not make the dinner, you understand, but some supports, if that would be helpful."

We agreed that it would be very helpful, though I did think I'd done a nice job with the cheeses.

"Excellent." Pierre raised his water glass. "As always, to a better tomorrow."

FIFTEEN

"Bonne journée" were the first words I heard the next morning.

Followed by a correction. "It is bun, not bone-y," Lia said.

"Bone jour-ney," Martin said.

"This is closer," Lia encouraged.

"Bonne journée," I said flawlessly from my cot.

Lia's face lit up, and she responded with a string of French words I didn't understand.

"Thank you," I said anyway. "What time is it?"

"En français, s'il vous plaît," Lia said.

"How . . . is . . . an . . . hour?" I said in French.

"What hour *is it?"* Lia corrected. "Ten."

"We are finishing our French vocabulary lesson," Martin said.

"His lesson," Lia said.

"*Merci, professeure*," Martin said. "But now that we are all awake, we can begin in the garden."

I looked over at Annie, who was asleep.

"She said to wake her at noon," Lia said. "She does her best work with twelve hours of rest."

"So do I," I said, laying my head back on my pillow.

"You have to get up," Lia said. "I need your help."

"As do I," Martin said.

When we got there, the French students were already working in their garden. Or at least Emile and Michel were busy watering and weeding, while Simone was chasing Wilder through rows of vegetables. I waved to him, but he wasn't paying attention.

Simone had chased him down and was playfully reaching for whatever he'd hidden behind his back. After a few attempts, he brought his closed palm to Simone's face and opened it. Inside was a bright pink rose.

"Your friend is having fun, no?" came a familiar voice from behind me.

Startled, I spun around. "What? Where did you come from?"

Pierre was sitting on a beat-up silver pail in the tall grass. "I have been waiting for your family. I want to introduce you to the goats."

Swinging his pail, Pierre led Lia, Martin, and me past the château's entrance gates, across the street, and toward a much-less-fancy chain-link fence.

"All of this land is owned by my family," he explained. He pointed to a house down the dirt road. "That is my sister's. She is away but has a horse that I take care of. It is an albino, so it cannot be in the sun." He pointed in the opposite direction to another faintly visible house. "My neighbor, the professional farmer, who I mention earlier. I own his house, but let him stay for free, because he is so helpful."

He recited the combination for the locker-style lock attached to the chain-link fence, flung open the gate, and announced, "And *this* is the wild zone."

Inside the wild zone was a large, drooping tree surrounded by rocks, and a gravel path rumbling with the sound of a minor stampede.

"Come in, come in, we must close the gate," Pierre commanded.

I wrapped my fingers around the links in the fence as fifteen goats, some with horns, skittered toward me. I closed my eyes and braced myself for impact. But no horns struck me. Instead, they just wanted to lick my shoes, lick my legs, lick my hands, and follow my every movement to get in more licks whenever they could.

"They have a favorite," Pierre said.

After all the salt was removed from the surface of my skin, the goats turned and ambled away.

"Are we milking *all* of these?" I asked, looking at Pierre's single bucket.

"No, no. These are the wild goats. They will not give you their milk. But we have two domesticated goats for milking, on loan from my neighbor. They are a little more shy."

He led us down the gravel path to a fork in the road. To the right was the cherry orchard. To the left was a wide-open meadow rimmed with trees. Feasting on dirt beneath one of the farthest trees were two thin almond-colored goats.

"Who wants to go first?" Pierre asked.

While the goats had been friendly to me so far, I wasn't thrilled by the thought of squeezing udders. But I didn't have to worry. Martin and Lia volunteered at the same time.

"Show me your hands," Pierre commanded.

Lia waved her fingers for inspection.

"I am sorry to say, but I think they are a little too small

for milking," Pierre said. "You could still be the helper, though. If—"

Martin spread his long fingers.

Pierre pointed to him. "The milker."

"I'll be the observer," I offered.

"You will get a chance to milk," Pierre said with a wink. He leaned down and started to whisper something into the nearest goat's ear. "This is Bijou," he told us softly. "She can get a little bit . . . full of stress, so I have let her know that you are amateurs but will treat her with care."

He motioned for Lia to take over and modeled what to do, tenderly massaging Bijou's fur and humming a sweet tune that Lia mimicked perfectly.

Martin squatted down and placed the silver pail beneath Bijou's udder.

"*Very* care-ful-ly," Pierre instructed. "Make a circle with this finger to the thumb. Good, and now place the circle on the tip, the—what do you call it in English?"

"Milk source?" Martin said.

At the sound of his voice, Bijou kicked her left leg backward, connecting with Martin's shoulder. He cursed in German, and Bijou kicked again.

"You must be calm," Pierre said. "You are speaking a little too harsh. You have to be soft, you know." He demonstrated by lightly whispering, "*I just need a little milk, my dear.*"

Martin tried to emulate Pierre, speaking as softly and delicately as he could. But Bijou became even more skittish, kicking over the bucket and knocking off Martin's glasses.

"Maybe I should try?" Lia offered.

"No. You are being a wonderful helper." Pierre looked toward me and indicated that I was to crouch behind the goat that had just defeated Martin with three swift kicks.

Lia resumed her tendering as I repositioned the pail beneath Bijou.

"*Gentle, gentle,*" Pierre whispered as I cautiously wrapped my hand around Bijou's teat and connected my index finger to my thumb. I closed my eyes and waited for a kick, but none came.

"Now, with the other fingers, do a quick squeeze and . . ."

I followed Pierre's instructions, and a jet of milk shot out like water from a hose.

"Good, good." He laughed. "You are a natural."

After a few more quick jolts of milk, she calmed, and we settled into a rhythm, the pail filling halfway before Bijou slowed to small spurts.

"*Thank you, Bijou,*" I whispered before rising from my crouch to light applause.

I bowed, pail in hand. "Who's ready for cereal?"

"Not cereal," Pierre said. "This is for ice cream. I will show you how to make it tomorrow. But we will need more milk." He looked at the other goat and back toward Martin. "Want to try again?"

"It would not be right," Martin said. "This is the job for Rylan."

SIXTEEN

We were off dinner duty that night, allowed to relax in the stables while the other group prepared the meal. Martin and Annie practiced their French conversational skills with Lia, who had resumed her role as the instructor.

They invited me to join them, but I was more interested in checking my email. It had now been two full days since I'd emailed my father, and there was no way he hadn't read it by now.

I carried my phone in my hand, volume up, waiting for a notification as I walked toward the bench outside Pierre's cottage.

ping

ping

ping

I rapidly unlocked my screen and discovered:

- an email from school
- an ad for new shoes
- an email from Mom

Dejected, I slunk onto the bench and opened Mom's email.

I know the internet connection is likely to be unreliable there and you may not get this right away, but I wanted to let you know how much I MISS YOU here at home. 😊 It's not the same without you, as you can imagine, and I've taken to talking to the walls (just kidding). I hope you are having fun with Wilder and making so many new friends and memories. I know that you have a lot on your mind, but please know that whatever you decide to do, I love you and support you. Don't work too hard and try every food you're offered!

xoxo bisou bisou

Love,

Mom

As I read through Mom's message with her voice in my head, tears rose in my eyes. I pictured myself across the dinner table from her—instead of alone on a bench in the near dark, the only sound the faint echo of Wilder laughing with his new friends—and became overwhelmed.

I hunched forward. Tears flowed down my nose, salting my lip. It wasn't just Wilder and my father ignoring me; it was the feeling that wherever I went, I would always be outside of the inner circle.

Somehow, Wilder could drop into a totally new social scene and figure it out instantly, just like he did at school. I'd never been able to do that. It was almost as if other people simply looked at me and saw something weird or wrong.

I thought things might be different in another country, but they weren't. Mom was the only one who really accepted me. But what else was she going to do—ditch me, too?

I tried to take deep breaths and control the negative path of my thoughts. As it had the morning before, Pierre's window popped open.

"Bad day?" he called.

"I'm okay." I sniffled. "Just a little homesick. I got an email from my mom."

"Ah, *mélancolie*," Pierre said. "'*C'est le bonheur d'être triste.*' Do you know who said this?"

"Someone French."

"Yes, Victor Hugo," Pierre said. "He is French."

"What does it mean?"

Pierre pondered for a moment. "In English it does not capture the feeling. But it sounds nice, no?"

"Could you say it again?"

Pierre recited the sentence like a proud poet. "'C'est le bonheur d'être triste.'"

"It's nice," I agreed, wiping a small line of snot on the cuff of my sweatshirt. I tried to collect myself as Pierre joined me outside. He fitted himself on the other side of the bench and lit a cigarette.

"You are not the first person to cry here," he said, pointing to the bench. "It is a normal thing to do. To be lonely away from your home."

At the sound of "lonely," I felt another surge in my throat and looked down.

"I will tell you a story," Pierre said. "When I was your age, I was accepted into a famous school in Paris. It was a military school, you see, and they are very cruel there. Yelling at you, tearing up your schoolwork if it is not precise. And every Friday I would write a letter to my mother, and I would say 'Please, take me home. This place is inhumane. I cannot be here another day.' Letter and letter and letter. And do you know what my mother writes? 'You cannot come home. Enjoy yourself.'" Story finished, he leaned back on the bench.

"And then you started enjoying yourself?" I prodded.

"No. I dropped out. The military is not for me."

"Then what's the point of the story?" I asked.

"It is normal to be lonely away from home." He took a drag on his cigarette. "And for mothers to insist that you enjoy yourself."

"I mean, I *am* enjoying myself sometimes," I said.

"You are not having fun with your bunkmates?"

"No, I am. I like all of them, it's just—"

As if on cue, laughter erupted from the kitchen.

"The other group seems to be having more fun," I said.

"I am not sure about *more* fun," Pierre said. "They are friends before. It can usually be a few days for the new SCOFFers to start being so friendly."

"Wilder seems to be their friend already."

"You know that you can join them whenever you prefer," Pierre said. "These groupings are not meant to be for all day long. You can do what you like."

"Really?"

"Of course. But I do think your group may be a little disappointed to lose you in their garden."

"And in the kitchen."

Pierre laughed. "Your cheese selection was the only acceptable dish."

"Was our meal really that bad?" I asked.

Pierre lowered his head. "To most French"—he pointed toward the students working on tonight's meal—"it is not acceptable. But it is okay. You will learn." He stubbed out his cigarette and crushed it under his heel. "As for missing your mother, I do have a landline."

"A what?"

"Am I really so old?" Pierre said with a shake of his head. "It is a telephone, you see?" He pointed to the window. Between the clutter on his desk rested an old telephone the color of an egg yolk.

"Ooohhh, like in seventies movies," I said. "Can I really call her?"

"If you would like," Pierre offered. "It is early in the US, but I do not mind paying for the long distance."

He led me inside and offered a brief dialing tutorial. Once the line started ringing, I gave Pierre a thumbs-up. He smiled and exited his room, closing the door behind him.

Mom answered groggily. "Hello?"

"Hi," I said, immediately followed by her "Oh, honey, I didn't know it was you. It showed up as this weird number. It's so good to hear from you. How are you?"

I tried to disguise the fact that I had started to tear up again at the sound of her voice. "I'm good. I'm really—"

"Are you sure? You sound a little . . . I don't know, *not* good?"

"I'm okay. I just . . . miss you," I said, my voice cracking at "miss."

"Sweetie," she said warmly. "It's okay. I'm always here, just a phone call or an email away."

"Thank you," I said. "I don't need anything. I just wanted to call and see what's going on. Did you go to the movies yesterday?"

"It was Monday night, wasn't it?" she said.

"What did you see?"

"You wouldn't have liked it. It was this French movie where everyone looks beautiful and has long conversations, but nothing really happens. I saw it in your honor. But who cares what I'm doing. How is the farm?"

"Um, it's okay so far."

"*Okay? You* called *me*, remember. You have to give some details. What's the best thing you've done so far?"

"I milked a goat this morning."

"You didn't."

"And caught wild bees. Good wild bees, not the bad ones."

"There are different kinds?"

"The bad ones can get too angry, at least that's what Pierre said."

"And how is he?"

"He's . . . nice. I mean, he's kind of weird, but he's, you know, letting me use his phone, and he made me coffee this morning, and he's going to teach me how to cook tomorrow, and make ice cream, and I think we're going to pick cherries."

"And you're missing *me*?"

I laughed into the receiver. Pierre knocked on the window and mimed eating with a spoon.

"Sorry, Mom, but I have to go."

"Time to make artisanal French ice cream?"

"That's tomorrow. The French students made dinner tonight."

"What an awful time you're having," she said sarcastically.

"I love you, Mom."

"I love you more." She smacked her lips next to the phone once. "Right cheek." And again. "Left cheek. Stop missing me and have fun."

I laid the receiver back on its resting dock and stepped outside. Pierre was still waiting for me on the bench. "Are you ready for a real French meal?" he asked.

I smiled at him.

"See," he said. "Now you are enjoying yourself."

SEVENTEEN

The next morning, I milked the goats on my own, dropped the pail in the kitchen, and picked up the latest edition of *Le Monde*, which Pierre had left out for me. While I mostly just looked at the pictures, I imagined myself as a sophisticated European, leisurely enjoying a croissant, pondering international news in the backyard of my summer home, taking in some sun before the day's work ahead.

In the movie version of this moment I would be wearing sunglasses and cool clothes, with a jazzy French song playing in the background. In reality, I wore the same jeans from yesterday and a blue T-shirt already stained with a spray of goat milk. I provided my own soundtrack by whistling a made-up song as I took out my phone for a cursory stop by the internet bench. There was only one notification this time.

It was the one I'd been waiting for.

My whistling fizzled. I stared at the blue dot to the left of my father's name, not wanting to look at the words he wrote, too nervous about what they might reveal. I put my phone back into my pocket and considered waiting until after breakfast. I started to walk back toward the kitchen, but then thought again. Taking a deep breath, I reopened my email and read: "Hey buddy, I can't tell you how great it is to hear from you. I know it's . . ."

Without bothering to sit down, I clicked through to read the full message.

. . . been a while and I haven't been the best at keeping in touch over the years. I spoke to your mother a little bit ago to see if maybe we could change that, and it looks like she finally passed that message along. But who would have thought that you'd be all the way over here? I wish you had told me in advance, though, because my time-line doesn't quite line up with yours. I already have an early morning flight booked for July 15 and I really can't miss it. I'm sorry to disappoint, buddy, but if there is any other time you would be free to meet before then, I'll try to make it there.

I hope you are enjoying France and all the French ways. It took me a while to get used to all the customs here, but I've settled in pretty nicely. I hope to hear from you soon.
All my best,
Dad

I read it again. And a third time. With each successive read, I felt worse. Despite all the attempts at being nice—the use of "buddy" and how much he really wanted to see me—the core message seemed to be *Sorry, I'm busy. Maybe next time.*

If this was what he'd really meant, the rest of it seemed fake—filled with the same "kind and considerate" words they made us use in school emails. But part of me couldn't accept this. Maybe he *was* busy on the exact day I'd asked to meet. Maybe he *was* serious about finding another time. If I talked to Pierre, maybe we *could* arrange something before the fifteenth?

I didn't have time to think. The rest of the farm was now awake; I could hear everyone congregating around the table, making plans for the day. I slid my phone into my pocket, tried to push the warring interpretations of my father's message to the back of my mind, and joined them.

The day's plan was to begin restoring the antique greenhouse. It was not possible, Pierre explained as he led us past the gardens, to fully restore it this summer, but he hoped we could at least clear out the weeds that had overtaken the interior and replace the missing glass on the roof.

"As you can see," Pierre said once we'd gathered next to the greenhouse, "there is quite a bit of glass gone missing."

The greenhouse, which was shaped like a small church, looked like those pictures of broken-down buildings in abandoned amusement parks. The roof was a metal skeleton where squares of glass used to connect. There were still a few rows of glass remaining, but most followed a pattern: glass, empty, empty, empty, glass, empty, empty.

"Lucky for us," Pierre continued, "I have received a donation of antique glass squares for the repair. Today we will clean the glass and count if we have enough. There are only so many buckets for washing, so you will need to pick a partner. One will *delicately* scrub. The other will *gently* dry."

I looked at Wilder, who, for the first time since we'd arrived, returned my gaze with a nod. It didn't escape my notice that Simone and Emile had already joined arms and Michel was considered the oddball of their group, but I wasn't going to complain. This was my chance to join their social circle.

"Look who needs a partner," I said, walking over to Wilder.

"Shut up," he said, but he was smiling a little. "Are you going to be the scrubber?"

"I thought that might be your job," I said.

"That's what you thought, huh?" he said.

"I know how much you enjoy scrubbing. I wouldn't want to take that away from you."

"Scrubbing *is* one of my passions, but I'm willing to let you try it just this once."

We both laughed and agreed to take turns. I went to fill our bucket and pick up the soap and rag from Pierre.

When I returned, Wilder had already situated himself next to Emile and Simone. I set down the bucket and said "It is washing time" in French, hoping to impress them.

Simone and Emile laughed, but not in the good way.

"*Laver* means wash, right?" I asked.

"*Oui*," Simone said. "But you are saying 'the washing machine has started.'"

"Are *you* the washing machine?" Emile teased.

I could feel my face reddening but tried to play along. I turned an imaginary washing machine dial, made a *whooshing* sound effect, and lowered a piece of glass into the bucket.

They all stared at me.

"Now it's started. The washing machine," I clarified.

Emile whispered something quickly in French. The only word I recognized was *étrange*, which means what it sounds like and is not something you want to be called.

"I was just joking," I said.

Wilder looked at Simone with an embarrassed smile. "I can take over the washing machine," he said.

"It's okay," I said, still holding the first piece of glass in the sudsy water. "I don't mind."

Emile pulled the first clean square of glass from his own bucket and handed it to Simone. She raised it to her face and scrutinized her reflection.

I lifted my glass square out of the water and saw that it was almost entirely clean except for a resistant black circle on one corner. I dunked it back in and scrubbed hard on the black circle until I felt a crack. My face flushed as two pieces of glass floated to the surface of the bucket.

"Did you—" Wilder started.

"It was an accident," I said.

"Problem with the washing machine?" Emile called.

"Shut up," I muttered, looking down at the broken glass.

"*Quel?*" Emile said.

I looked Emile in the eyes. "I said 'Shut up.'"

"He doesn't mean it," Wilder said to Emile.

"I do mean it," I said.

"Come on," Wilder said. "This isn't a big deal."

"I agree," Emile said. "It is not a big deal that your washing machine is not working."

"I made one mistake," I said.

"Then why don't you try to clean another one?" Emile taunted.

"Fine," I said.

I picked up a new piece of glass and dipped it into the water. But the anger coursing through me was too great. Within seconds came another muffled crunch of glass.

It was one of those moments when I wished I really was a character in a movie. A character with the ability to stop time. I knew what was coming: Emile would continue taunting, Simone would laugh, and Wilder would look slightly embarrassed for me, but more for his connection to me, worried that this would tarnish his reputation with his new friends. And I'd be alone at the center of it all, trying not to act like a little kid, not to burst into tears or run away in a huff.

But of course, time didn't stop. Instead, everything happened at once. I looked down at the water, which was tinged red from a cut on my thumb, and mumbled something about needing to go wash my hands. Stiffly and self-consciously I walked past everyone until I was out of sight. Then I began to run toward the restroom next to the stable.

My left hand was red with blood. I turned on the rickety faucet and felt the sting of ice-cold water as it splashed the red away. Wrapping my hand in toilet paper, I sat down on the seat and, for the second time in two days, started to cry. This time no one was around, so I didn't try to limit myself.

By the time I'd moved into hiccupping and sniffling, I knew that nothing had been resolved. I was no closer to Wilder, to meeting my father, to going home—but still, I felt slightly better. Not good enough to return to the greenhouse, but enough to leave the restroom and walk over to the stable, where I hoped to lie down for a while. Rewrapping my hand with a string of toilet paper, I stepped through the entrance, only to find that I wasn't alone. Martin was hunched over his notebook with a protractor and a chipped golf pencil.

"Oh, hey, aren't you . . ." I started.

He didn't look up from his work. "The trench construction plan is nearly finished."

"That's great." I sat down on my cot. "Is everyone else still down at the greenhouse?"

"Everyone . . . except . . . me," Martin said distractedly.

Then, satisfied with his final sketch, he closed his notebook. "My partner, Michel, was confident in his ability to both wash and dry the glass, so I asked if I could leave to work on my plan."

"That's nice of him," I said.

"He does seem to be of the nicer kind," Martin said. "More so than the others."

"Yeah, they weren't being the nicest kind."

"I heard a little bit of it," Martin said.

"I broke some glass," I said.

"This happens with glass," Martin said.

"And they were teasing me a little."

"And you injured yourself?"

I held up my hand. A small circle of blood had formed on the toilet paper. "It wasn't that bad."

"There is no one here," Martin said conspiratorially. "You can complain."

I looked toward the door.

"See? No one," Martin said. "I could start if you would like. Your friend Wilder is a *rotzlöffel*."

I started cracking up at the sound of the word.

"You know this word?" he asked.

I shook my head.

"It is like a spoon filled with, um, what is this called?"

He pointed to the inside of his nose.

"Nose hair?"

"No. The liquid, the slime."

"Snot."

"Ah, yes. It is a spoon of snot," Martin explained. "You say this for someone who is trying to be a cool guy." He mimed sticking up his nose and acting cool. "But up his nose is actually all of this *snot*, which we can see."

This made me laugh even harder.

"Why are you always acting so nervous around him?" Martin asked.

"I'm not nervous around him," I said.

"You broke the glass," he said. "You are always looking at him to check what he is doing at dinner."

"It's not him." I rubbed my bandaged hand. "I mean, it is, but it's not just him."

Martin looked at me, waiting for me to continue.

"It's a long story," I said.

"As I was saying, we are alone. I am finished with my plan. There is nothing else for us to do."

I wasn't used to anyone besides my mom offering to listen to me, and even she had her limits before trying to steer me toward her point of view. I told Martin what I knew about my father, the email I sent, and how he responded.

Martin didn't offer any assurances or share his opinion on what I should do. Instead he said, "This is a very difficult situation. I am sorry you are inside of it."

"Yeah," I said. "I mean, thank you."

"You do not need to thank me. I have done nothing."

"You listened."

"It is what a friend does," he said. "Is Wilder not like this?"

"I haven't exactly told him. He knows about my father, obviously, but not anything else. He actually . . ." I trailed off, unsure if I wanted to tell him about the slideshow, about the picture Wilder added.

"He actually . . ." Martin prompted.

"I don't think he really cares."

"And yet he is your friend?" Martin said skeptically. "Is it like this with all Americans?"

"Maybe," I said. "Probably. I'm not really sure."

"It is not like this with Germans. If we are not being friendly to each other, then we stop being friends. It is a matter of choice. A decision that you make."

"You just decide to stop being friends and then you aren't friends anymore?"

"Yes, it is like this," he said. "When I was like you, in

grade seven, it was a similar situation with Wilder as I had with two friends. They were not wanting to sit with me, spending more of their time with the girls. At the end of the year, we have a big dance, and they say it is okay, it will be fun, we can all go together. But when we arrive, it is the same as it has been before. They are laughing and they are jumping, and I want to have fun too, but I cannot. I watch everyone dance and I wait for the beat to come for me. To cheer me. To lift me from where I was feeling. But I did not feel it. I felt nothing. I was only standing."

"I'm sorry," I said.

"It is okay now," Martin said.

"But it wasn't then."

"No, it was not okay for a few weeks. But that night I made the decision to stop being their friend."

"Did you find new friends?" I asked.

"I am still trying." Martin looked down. "That is part of why I am here."

"You're doing a pretty good job so far," I said.

He looked back up. "You think so?"

"You're the best friend I have here," I said.

"Does this mean we are friends?"

"I just made the decision," I said.

Martin beamed. And so did I.

"No more breaking glass now," he said.

"I hope so," I said.

"Have you made your other decision?" he asked.

"Not yet, but I have some time. He waited three days to write back to me. Plus ten years before that. I think I have a few days to respond."

EIGHTEEN

That night was our first cooking lesson. After the cus-tomary three-hour rest in the middle of the afternoon, Annie, Lia, Martin, and I met Pierre in the kitchen. He had already laid out an assortment of vegetables and a large chicken and was flipping through a ringed collection of yellowed index cards.

"I am only somewhat of a chef," Pierre said. "But my mother was a"—he kissed his fingers—"*cuisinère merveilleuse*. Many delicious recipes she has left behind."

He selected three index cards and set them on the counter. "We will start with *artichokes à la barigoule*. Step one is to take out the heart."

"That sounds violent," Annie said.

"It is beautiful," Pierre said, handing her a knife. He laid an artichoke in front of each of us as we lined up side by side along the kitchen counter.

Following his lead, we each cut the top and then the sides and then the stem, leaving just the base, which was the heart of the artichoke. I looked down the counter to see four perfectly cut artichoke hearts on each of our cutting boards and felt a tiny bubble of pride.

Pierre collected the hearts and put them into a bowl of cold water. He gave us each a vegetable—carrots, onions, garlic, and leeks—and, one by one, described how they should be cut. Flying high on the artichoke heart success, Lia bounced up and down next to me while cutting her carrots.

"Now we take this." Pierre picked up a box of matches, leaned down, and lit a burner on the stove. "And this." He placed a pot atop the flame. "Splash in this." He poured in a generous amount of cooking wine, spaced out the artichokes, and then lined the remaining bottom of the pot with the cut vegetables. "Allow for it to sit. Twenty minutes—done!"

Pierre picked up the soup recipe card and quickly scanned it.

"This one will be even more easy. We need somebody to cut the potatoes and the others to make the *mirepoix*."

"*Mirepoix?*" Annie repeated.

"You do not know it?" Pierre asked.

We all, somewhat ashamedly, shook our heads. Pierre was astonished.

"It is the *foundation* for French cooking! Charles-Pierre-Gaston François de Lévis, duc de Lévis-Mirepoix. This is *nothing* to you?"

Hearing the Frenchest name of all time was notable but otherwise meant nothing to us.

Pierre had to calm himself down. "Okay. It is okay. That is why you are here—to learn."

He demonstrated how to dice each vegetable into roughly the same size. After we had made three rows of green, white, and orange vegetables, Annie pushed them together to resemble a flag.

"Look, it is India," she said.

"Or the Ivory Coast," Lia said.

"Or Ireland," I said.

"It is France," Pierre said, scooping the vegetables into a pot.

We glanced at one another and giggled, but Pierre was too absorbed in concocting the perfect *mirepoix* to notice.

"Now that we have the base," Pierre said, "we need the potato. Many potatoes. This one you will do together as I prepare the chicken."

We diced the potatoes, and Pierre poured cooking wine into another sizzling pot on the stove before laying down strips of chicken. The aromas of the *mirepoix*, artichoke hearts, and chicken mixed in the air, and I momentarily imagined myself as an apprentice chef behind the kitchen doors of a fancy restaurant. In this scene I was just on potato duty, wearing a hairnet, but only because it was my first week and the head chef was testing me. If I cut the potatoes to his exact specifications, he would reward me with a chef's hat.

Pierre did compliment my pile of potatoes, but no chef's hat was offered. We set the table while he finished making the main meal.

When we returned, he pulled a metal bowl out of the freezer and placed it inside a larger white plastic bowl with a handle and a faded sticker depicting a yellow ice cream cone and the word *Donvier*.

Pierre tapped the sticker. "This is an original Japanese ice cream maker from 1975. My father bought it in Japan and used it all the time."

"He doesn't use it anymore?" I asked.

"He passed away many years ago. The day I was born, he was flying his own plane to the hospital, and he did not make it down." Though he had clearly said this many times before, there was still a ring of emotion in Pierre's voice. I stifled the urge to give him a hug. Too American.

He lifted the contraption into the air. "But his ice cream maker is still here, and it remains the best in the world. I will show you his recipe."

Pierre called out the ingredients, and we gathered them. Fresh goat's milk! Butter! Two eggs! Several spoonfuls of sugar! A dash of vanilla! After whisking it all together in the bowl, Pierre tossed in a handful of cherries.

"All that remains is the turning," Pierre said. "As the man who secured the milk, I think it is only right for the job to go to Rylan."

He graciously stepped aside. I turned the plastic knob at the top of the ice cream mixer until the ingredients swirled together.

Pierre returned to the stove and lifted the top from the pot of *poulet basquaise*. "*This* is a French dinner." He wafted the delightful smells that rose from the pot. "If it tastes as good as it smells, we can make it again for our special guest on Saturday."

"Special guest?" I asked.

"A friend from the Jardin du Luxembourg in Paris. They call him the Rose Whisperer. He will be coming to whisper to our roses. In return, he will expect a nice meal."

"You really trust us to make a nice meal?" I asked.

"Of course," Pierre said. "You just did."

NINETEEN

On paper, Martin's trench plan looked simple. Between each row of vegetables was a long, thin rectangle labeled *Trench*, with numbers marking the neighboring vegetables' average root lengths. But creating long trenches involved hours and hours of plunging shovels into hard dirt and slowly making smaller holes into smooth pathways.

I was on digging duty, along with Martin, and had to work around a blister on my hand that had bloomed after the first day. Lia was the inspector of insects and roots—carefully guiding us from severing either with our shovels. Annie tried to shovel a few times but didn't get very far. Instead, she appointed herself in charge of the trench aesthetics. When we finished digging, she went through with a trowel, ensuring that the lines were straight and the depth equal throughout.

It took us three full days to finish. By the end of day three, we all collapsed on the grass next to our newly organized *schrebergarten*. Everyone, that is, except for Martin, who explained that it was now time to fill the trenches.

"You mean we're not *done*?!" I huffed.

"Trenches are only useful if they are filled," Martin said plainly.

"You could have said that before."

"I thought it was an implication."

"It wasn't clear to me," I said.

"Or to me," Annie said. "I like its current look. It's clean. Symmetrical. I don't want to dirty it up with banana peels or fish skeletons or whatever."

"We do not need these things. This is not a cartoon," Martin said. "We need things like the grass we collected, or scraps of food, the hay from the stable, and maybe some of the goat, um"—Martin made a mound with his hands—"deposits."

"Turds," I said.

"*Scheisse*, yes."

"You want us to collect goat turds?" I said.

Martin smiled. "To enrich the trenches."

"We could collect bird droppings, too," Lia said. "It will

attract earthworms—which also enrich the soil."

"I did not know this," Martin said excitedly.

"I used bird droppings to attract insects when I built my insect hotel," Lia said.

"You made a *hotel* for *insects*?" Annie said.

"Everyone in Switzerland does so in third grade," Lia said matter-of-factly.

Annie's eyes sparkled. "With tiny doors and little beds?"

"It was not this kind of hotel," Lia said. "But I won the top prize!"

"Hotel Manager of the Year," Annie said.

Lia smiled. "I still have the hotel. And I collect more insects each year."

"Is there another contest coming up?" Annie asked.

"No, not really. No one is very interested in insects in my grade anymore." The smile disappeared from Lia's face.

"*We* are interested," Annie said.

"I love insects," I lied. "And I know where we can get some bird droppings, too."

All eyes turned toward me. I pointed to the castle. We had all watched the same introduction video, and the realization slowly dawned on everyone.

Annie leaped up excitedly. "Finally! I have been waiting all week to go inside the castle!"

"We *could* do this, but"—Martin hesitated—"I have

a bit of a phobia about being inside a castle with"—he paused and lowered his voice—"*wild birds*."

"You are afraid of *birds*?" Annie said.

Martin waved his hands in a "lower your voice" gesture, as if he were scared that nearby birds would hear his secret. "I have several times had a nightmare about being attacked by a group of birds."

"Like in *The Birds*?" I asked. Every December, Mom's and my favorite theater showed Alfred Hitchcock movies on the big screen, and *The Birds* played last year.

Martin looked at me strangely. "You've seen it?"

"Yeah, it's great."

"My father showed me this film when I was young," Martin said. "Too young. And since then, well—"

"But that is only a movie," Annie said.

I agreed. "These birds won't peck your eyes out." (Which is what happens in *The Birds*. They also peck people in the throat, set a gas station on fire, and destroy an entire town. As I said, it's a great movie.)

"There is no guarantee," Martin said.

"I can protect you," I said.

"Me too," Annie and Lia said at the same time.

Martin resignedly agreed, and we quickly hatched a plan.

He would stay on the ground floor while the rest of

us spread out to the upper levels. We each carried a tool to scrape bird droppings from the floor (for me, a garden trowel) and a bucket in which to deposit them. These were the same buckets we'd used to clean glass back at the greenhouse. For me, they were still charged with negative associations, so I was looking forward to flinging bird poop into them.

We walked over to the castle, and Annie pulled the door open. From inside came an agitated rustling. Then, four loud splats onto the floor.

Martin gripped my arm, terrified. I pinched my nose, disgusted. Lia scooped up the fresh bird deposit, pleased.

From our view in the entryway, it was obvious that our original plan wouldn't work. The staircases were in different stages of rot, and none were safe to climb. The floor, having served as a bird toilet for decades, was crusted over like the paint palette of an artist who worked with only dark grays and greens.

Above us, pigeons perched from every railing and window. It *was* very much like the movie *The Birds*, except these pigeons were husky. It was difficult to imagine them swiftly swooping down to pluck out Martin's eyes, though they did appear to be tracking our every footstep past the front door.

We waited a few moments, unsure when the next rain would fall and not wanting it to land in our hair. When the coast seemed clear, Annie and Lia tiptoed to the left. I walked to the right, Martin close behind me, like a child hiding behind his mother's skirt.

"*I. Must. Exit,*" he whispered.

"*Let's just go a little farther,*" I whispered back.

"*I can hear them plotting,*" he said.

"*They're cooing.*"

"*It is a coo with menace.*"

A particularly plump pigeon rustled its wings above us. Martin shot me a pointed look.

"Two more minutes," I said.

We crept into what used to be a living room. Above a mantel worn to bits of wood was a painted portrait of a man in a nineteenth-century military uniform. He looked shockingly similar to Pierre, the only difference a small hole in his left cheek. From my research, I knew this was Pierre's great-great-uncle, and the small hole was where a bullet had passed through when he'd stepped in front of Napoleon.

I set down my bucket and trowel and fished my phone out of my pocket.

"*What are you doing?*" Martin whispered.

"*I want to take a picture.*"

"*I do not think the birds will like it,*" he protested.

"*My flash is off.*"

And it was. But my sound, unfortunately, was on. At the click of the camera, a calamity of flapping rang through the castle.

"Retreat!" Martin yelled.

Birds began dropping from the ceiling like bombs. Martin tripped over his bucket, his glasses skidding across the floor.

"I can't see!" he shouted.

As he frantically felt around the crusted floor, a pigeon landed on his back with a thud. Martin shrieked and rolled around as if he were on fire. The bird slammed into the wall.

"This is my exact nightmare!" he screamed from the floor.

The shaken pigeon began waddling toward him as he scampered up. I hopped over the bird and scooped up Martin's glasses, then caught up to him and pressed them into his hand. As promised, I shielded him the rest of the way as birds nose-dived toward the ground floor.

Annie and Lia leaped out the front door just ahead of us. I slammed it shut, pressing my back into the wood and panting.

Martin kept running through the open field. Annie and

Lia doubled over laughing, and I joined them, giddy from our escape.

"I guess Martin was right," I said.

Lia agreed. She lifted her mostly empty bucket, and said, "I suppose we have to go collect goat droppings after all."

"Have fun with that," Annie said.

"You're not helping?" I asked.

"I am finished with feces for the day," she said. "But the castle has inspired me. I'm headed to the greenhouse. To paint." She took off in her version of a rush. That is, very slowly, but in a straight line rather than lackadaisically.

I sighed and looked at Lia.

"Inspiration cannot be interrupted," she said.

I was not inspired to collect goat turds, but somebody had to. Lia and I walked over to the wild zone, squatting and scooping until the sun went down. Martin eventually joined us, and just before dinner we had enough manure to spread through every trench.

TWENTY

I slept in later than ever the next morning, so tired from filling the trenches that I missed breakfast. But not so tired that I skipped goat milking. When I opened the gate to the wild zone, I expected a few goats to come rushing over as usual, but none were in sight.

Instead, I heard voices: Wilder and the French students. It sounded like they were doing some actual work in the cherry orchard. I didn't want to join them, but I had to pass them on the way to the goats. I tried to walk as quietly as possible. But then I heard my name.

I froze.

"He's not that bad or anything," Wilder was saying.

"He is an *annoyance* to you," Emile prodded.

"He can be *annoying*, yeah," Wilder said. "Everyone can be annoying, but it's more just like he doesn't get it."

I felt my heart squeeze. Part of me wanted to tiptoe away, knowing that whatever he said next would be more than I wanted to hear. But the other part of me wanted to know how he really felt. I pressed my back against a tree and braced for the truth.

"We're not seven anymore. I don't care about watching movies and making up stories and stuff. I want to *do things*, with other people. Go to parties."

"We should have a party here," Simone suggested.

"If we did, he would try to be by my side the whole time. Or watching me while I'm talking to other people. I just get sick of it."

"Anyone would get sick," Emile said.

I was starting to get sick.

"The only reason I invited him is because my mom made me."

I knew it. My legs started trembling. But soon the sickness and trembling passed, and I just felt sad. Sad and, weirdly, some sense of . . . relief.

Now I knew I hadn't been making things up. There was never a real truce between us. There never would be.

"I feel lucky that *we* got put together," Wilder said. "And he's with all the other weirdos."

"To the fates!" Emile called.

"*Les jardiniers suprêmes!*" Michel roared, and they devolved into celebrating the nickname they had given themselves.

I used the commotion as my chance to slip away, grasping tightly to the handle of the milking pail and walking into the long grass of the goat field to find Bijou.

She skittered over as soon as she saw me. I crouched down and petted her on the top of her head.

"*You're my friend, aren't you, Bijou?*" I whispered into her ear.

She mewed pleasantly, and I was happy to focus all of my mental energy on the task of milking rather than attending to my own thoughts.

But as with all brains, mine wouldn't let me avoid the sentences it played in a loop:

You knew Wilder didn't like you anymore.

No one really likes you.

No one will ever like you.

A week ago, these thoughts would have overwhelmed me. I would have kept repeating what Wilder said, letting each repetition cut me more deeply until I felt completely worthless.

But today I thought of Bijou, and escaping from the

castle, and learning to make ice cream, and talking to Martin in the stable.

I whispered a thank-you to Bijou, lifted the half-filled bucket, and carried it back to the kitchen, where I was surprised to find Annie bent over the sink, washing two tiny paintbrushes. She jumped at the sound of my pail hitting the floor.

"Sorry," I said.

"You just scared me is all."

"You're up earlier than usual."

"You are up late." She laid the paintbrushes next to the sink and turned to face me. "*And* you missed the major announcement at breakfast."

"The Rose Whisperer is coming tomorrow? I already know."

"No. Well yes, he is, but the even *larger* announcement." Annie paused dramatically. "Pierre has agreed to put *me* in charge of the greenhouse repair."

I started lightly clapping.

"And," she continued, "he said I could do whatever I want."

"Which is . . ."

"Let me show you," Annie said.

She gave me a moment to pour the milk from the pail

into a glass jar, and then led me toward the greenhouse. I hadn't been there since the glass-breaking incident, and I was impressed by how much it had changed. All the glass squares had been cleaned and organized into tidy piles. Several squares had already been fitted back into the empty metal frames, and the interior had been cleared of weeds and transformed into Annie's art studio.

She had built an impromptu easel out of old wooden drawers, found a can of white paint, and unpacked a miniature watercolor set that seemed intended for young children.

"They are the only painting materials I could fit safely in my luggage," she explained. "And anyway, I only use these watercolors for practice." She pointed to the floor, where she had painted several versions of the morning sky across the pages of yesterday's *Le Monde*. Half were crumpled up.

I bent down and uncrumpled them. "You're just throwing these away?" I asked, impressed by the colors she was able to wring out of her tiny watercolor kit.

"I am practicing like the French," Annie said. "Possibly it is a legend, but I learned that Renoir and Cézanne used to paint a few watercolors in the morning to warm up. To get their artistic energy flowing. Then they would crumple them and light a fire to keep themselves warm for the rest of the day and into the night. I would not light a fire in here because everything would burn down immediately, but I can keep to the same basic principle."

"If this is just your warm-up, then what's the main project?" I asked.

Annie picked up her phone. "As you've probably noticed, I have been taking photos of the sky each day."

I had seen her doing this a few times, but I didn't know it was every day.

"This was more for fun in the beginning," Annie said. "The sky is so beautiful here, and the clouds so . . . fluffy and big. It's not like this in Hong Kong all the time. Sometimes, yes, but often it's difficult to see the sky in full from where I live."

"You should see California skies."

"I would love to!" Annie enthused. "But anyway, yesterday, inside the castle, when I looked up and saw all the birds, there was one window that was uncovered. Through that window was the most perfect cloud. So perfect it looked like it was painted on the glass."

She set down her phone and lifted one of the cleaned glass squares. "You are following?"

"Not exactly . . ."

"My idea is to paint one sky for every day."

"On the glass squares?"

"Yes, on the glass. Simply, just using white paint to show the clouds."

"Are there thirty different clouds you could paint?"

Annie looked confused, or maybe offended. "There are millions, infinite. No cloud is ever the same as another cloud. It only looks that way."

I was surprised into silence.

"Do you like it?" she asked eagerly.

"It sounds . . . amazing."

Her face glowed.

"And when I am finished," she said. "When I have twenty or so squares done, I will mix them in with the rest of the clean glass. Then there will always be a record of what the clouds were like when I was here. And if you were to come back in ten years, let's say, you could still see the clouds from ten years ago and compare them to the new reflections of clouds from that day."

Whatever feelings of betrayal and disappointment I felt earlier were now completely gone. *Les jardiniers suprêmes* could have their lazy cherry picking, their perfect garden and nice bedrooms. I was happy to be with the "weirdos."

TWENTY·ONE

The Rose Whisperer (who preferred to be called by his real name, Jules) arrived at noon, wearing a spotless white smock with four pockets. In each pocket was a different cutting tool, none named "scissors," though all looked like scissors to some degree. He lined them up neatly on the dining table before sitting down for a two-hour talk about the "metaphysical life of the rose."

The lecture was mostly in French and very difficult for me to follow, even when he spoke in English. Rather than contributing my thoughts (which were *what??*), I took on the role of a waiter, bringing out more bread and cheese and refilling water glasses. This made me feel useful and seemed to delight Jules, who ate an entire block of cheese on his own.

After lunch, Pierre led Jules and the rest of us through the rose patch. To my eyes, the roses seemed to be in pretty good shape. A little messy, maybe, but there were certainly a lot of them in different effulgent colors.

Jules placed a tiny pair of glasses on the crook of his nose and pressed his face closely to each rose, then bent down to trace it to its roots. He said nothing to us throughout the process, and I didn't hear any whispering to the roses either. When he finished his inspection, he tucked his glasses back into his smock.

"You have a *good* garden here. But!" He raised his index finger dramatically. "I am here to teach you how to create a *magnificent* garden." He extended his hands like an orchestra conductor. "For the rules of the garden are not just for the rose, but also for life."

Jules lectured animatedly for the next hour. Though he moved between English and French, and I didn't catch everything, I did my best to connect the literal rose garden lessons to their metaphorical life lessons:

1. Water the roses as early as possible each morning. *Get up early and take a shower.*

2. Inspect for bugs daily and use your hands to shoo them away. *Watch out for the people who are trying to bring you down and try to stop them before they eat all your metaphorical leaves.*

3. Rather than fertilizer, spread garlic at the base of rosebushes. *This just applies to roses, I think.*

4. When pruning, be precise in every cut you make. *Don't make a big change without thinking about it first.*

5. Do not be afraid to cut the stems not producing buds. *If something you're doing isn't working, it's okay to stop doing it.*

While lecturing, he also made cuts to each rosebush. These were his real whisperings—careful attention to each flower, which led to a small change, which helped it to prosper. With these slight alterations, he said, the roses would flourish by the middle of the summer.

Roses trimmed and lessons learned, Jules then walked through our garden to offer his assessment.

"What are you putting into these . . . what do you call them?" he asked.

"Trenches," Martin said. "Goat deposits, vegetable excess, these kinds of things."

"Good, good," Jules said. "You might also try some fish food."

"Do you mean algae?" Lia asked.

"No, no, like a—" Jules tried to form the word with his hands.

"Pellets," I said.

"Yes, the little ones from a pet shop. I have heard that this works. We cannot use this in Paris because it would bring out the cats, but here—"

"Can we add it to the grocery list?" Lia asked Pierre.

"There is a pet store in town," Pierre said. "You could get it for yourself if you like."

"How?" Lia asked.

"It is only five miles away," Pierre said. "I can show you the map after dinner, which . . ."

Like a seasoned waiter, he explained the evening's menu. Jules thrilled to the detailed description of each dish, and I began to doubt we'd be able to pull it off. Sure, we had improved since our first day, but we were hardly world-class chefs.

It took a few hours, some of Pierre's mother's most prized (though simple) recipes, and some burnt fish that didn't make it to the table, but the finished *coq au vin* was cooked to tender perfection. The roasted potatoes were soft and sweet, the fresh vegetables expertly mixed into a salad. Jules ate seconds and snuck some thirds while he sipped on the cele-bratory wine that Pierre had hand-selected for his visit.

"Can I say a toast?" Jules rose from his seat. "It is a most wonderful day here today. Thank you to all of the young people for being so inviting, and for helping to pre-pare this delicious meal. I lift up my glass *to you*."

Pierre lifted his wineglass while the rest of us lifted our water.

"No, no," Jules said. "We must do this proper. Everyone gets a wine."

Emile leaped out of his seat to bring wineglasses for all of us. Pierre did the honors, pouring small drops of wine into each glass in relation to our age. Lia got a drop no larger than a spoon of medicine. I was served the size of a dentist's rinse cup (but this would be much better than the dentist's water, I hoped).

We all stood with raised glasses.

"*À votre santé!*" Jules exclaimed.

I tipped back my wineglass. It tasted like very sour grape juice, and I knew I was making a disgusted face by the way Jules was laughing.

"Another toast!" Emile called, raising his empty glass in the air.

"One sip is enough," Pierre said, though he refilled his and Jules's glasses.

"As a return for your *hospitality*," Jules said, "I would like to invite you to visit me in Paris. We are having a special celebration *au Jardin du Luxembourg* for Bastille Day, and it would be my great pleasure for you to come and spend the day and night."

Bastille Day was on my list of French Things Mom Says I Need to Know, so I knew that it was the celebration of the French Revolution and always fell on the same day: July 14—aka the last day my father would be in Paris before leaving on his own trip.

"All of us?" I asked eagerly.

"Probably not all," Jules said. "I have one extra bedroom."

Pierre's eyes twinkled. "A decision for the fates."

"No," I said too loudly, and everyone's attention swung toward me. "I mean, I think it might be better if we decide some other way. The fates haven't always been kind to me."

Annie, Lia, and Martin looked hurt by my response, so I tried to clarify. "The fates have been kind to me here, but not elsewhere."

Everyone looked confused.

"Could we maybe just do something else to decide?" I pleaded.

"Do you have a suggestion?" Pierre asked.

"We could do a . . . uh . . . contest?" I said unconfidently.

"I like it," Wilder said.

"How about a raffle?" Lia suggested.

"How is that different from the fates?" Martin asked.

"I think a contest could be okay," Emile offered.

The rest of the table slowly grumbled their assent, though Pierre seemed skeptical.

"How would a contest work?" he asked.

"You said there was a festival at the end of the summer where you always have a stand, right?" I asked Pierre.

Pierre nodded.

"Then how about instead of one stand, we have two stands. One for them"—I gestured to *Les jardiniers suprêmes*—"and one for us. Whoever sells the most, whatever—fruit, vegetables, flowers—wins."

"It is very capitalistic, no?" Pierre said.

"You are a capitalist," Jules responded.

"In theory, yes, but—" Pierre started.

"In reality as well," Jules said, waving his arm to indicate Pierre's massive inherited property.

"And it would help your reputation with the other farmers," I said, "if you have *two* thriving stands."

"Our stand might not be thriving," Martin warned.

I kicked him under the table. Pierre did not seem to register Martin's remark. His mouth curled into a smile. "You really think so?"

"Of course," I said, using one of Pierre's most popular phrases.

"This is what everyone would like?" he asked the table.

Everyone nodded or shrugged. Then Lia raised her hand. "I have a question, though. Who gets the cherries?"

"We have picked the cherries," Emile said.

"I have picked *some* cherries," Martin said.

"We have picked the *most* cherries," Emile countered.

"You can *both* sell the cherries," Pierre said.

"How about the bees? Will there be honey in time for the festival?" I asked.

"Yes, probably," Pierre said.

"Then we get the honey," I said.

Wilder's hand shot up. "I helped with the bees."

Pierre and I exchanged looks, and then both stared at Wilder.

"Okay, fine," he relented.

"This is becoming a nice contest already," Jules said.

"All that remains is the handshake to guarantee the terms," Pierre said.

"Does everyone need to shake everyone else's hand?" Wilder asked.

"We can all join hands," Pierre said. "Like a prayer."

I reached to my left and right, joining hands with Martin and Annie.

Every hand at the table holding another, Pierre laid out the terms: "Of the two groups here today, one sitting on my right, and one sitting on my left, whoever sells the most at the Dreux Summer Festival will travel to Paris on the fourteenth of July for the Bastille Day celebration and stay the night at the residence of Jules in the *bourgeoisie* sixth arrondissement. If you agree, shake now."

All our arms swung up and down in agreement. The contest was on, and I was determined that we would win.

TWENTY·TWO

We planned to leave for the pet store at ten a.m. There was just one road and we would recognize the nearest town, Pierre said, when we saw buildings that sold things. After five miles, if we didn't reach buildings where things were available for purchase, we had somehow made a mistake.

Ten o'clock was early for everyone else, but not for me. I had already been over to the wild zone to milk Bijou and to the internet bench to email my father. This time I didn't hem and haw or go into details of how *maybe* I was going to be able to make it to Paris on the fourteenth. I told him I would be there for the entire day and could meet at any time.

I was certain we would win the contest, because I had a secret plan.

From my intensive hour of research that morning I had learned that the amount of milk Bijou produced was tied to what she ate. Currently, she ate grass, dirt, hay, tree bark, small rocks, and whatever else stuck to her tongue. After a few days, there was usually enough milk to fill several cereal bowls.

But if Bijou had some real goat food, the kind hopefully sold at a pet store five miles away, there would be enough milk to make cheese. Fresh, handmade goat cheese had to be worth *something* at the summer festival.

I was finishing my research when the rest of the crew assembled around the internet bench to check the map.

"Who's ready to hike?" I said with enthusiasm.

"Hike?" Annie repeated groggily.

"There is a little up and down," Martin confirmed, looking at the map. "But it does appear to be a straight line into town."

Annie did not look pleased.

"We can stop along the way," I reassured her.

"If we must," Martin conceded. He slipped the map into the fanny pack he wore around his waist. "A quick check for provisions before we depart: We all have money, yes?"

"I don't," Lia said.

"Why not?" Martin asked.

"I don't *have* money," Lia said. "I have never been given money."

"How will you buy lunch?" Martin said.

"We're buying lunch?" I asked.

Martin smiled. "I thought it would be nice."

"I can pay for you," Annie told Lia.

I had about 125 euros and hoped that was enough for goat food and lunch, a ticket to Paris, and dinner there, and . . . maybe I would need more money. But I at least expected to make it through the day without emptying my wallet.

"Sunscreen?" Martin asked, removing a tube of German sunscreen from his fanny pack and offering it around. Then he put on a wide-brimmed hat, smiled, and told us it was time to depart.

The walk there was mostly downhill and therefore easy. I knew the opposite would be true for the return trip, but I chose not to think about it, instead enjoying the cool wind and barren roads. We passed field after field, some stacked high with newly delivered hay, others largely empty, with a few grazing cattle. As we walked, Martin provided the soundtrack with his old iPod and mini speakers. He started with German techno music, but after we argued that it didn't fit the vibe of an early-morning walk, he changed to classical music—still German and bombastic but slower and more suited to our walking pace.

When we passed a sign informing us that we were one mile from town, Martin cut the music. "Before we arrive, we should develop a strategy," he said. "This is most likely our only opportunity to take the advantage in the contest."

"Do you really think we can win?" Lia said.

"Absolutely!" I said enthusiastically while Annie quietly said, "No."

"I think there is a possibility," Martin said calmly. "*If* we develop a strategy."

"I have a strategy," I said. "Or at least a few ideas."

"I am listening," Martin said.

"With the vegetables, we're about even with the other group," I started.

"Not quite," Martin said. "I don't know if Lia has shared this with you, but we walked through the garden this morning and noticed a number of aphids. Much more than are in the other *schrebergarten*."

"Meaning?" I asked.

"Meaning that these aphids are attaching themselves to the leaves of the vegetables and will slowly take out all of their sap."

"Which is what aphids are meant to do," Lia added.

"But still it is a problem," Martin said.

"Isn't that what the fish pellets are for?" I said.

"Those will improve the quality of nutrients in the soil, but will not affect the aphids," Martin said. "It is possible that at the store they will have some sort of *solution*—"

"We are not buying a pesticide," Lia said.

"I did not say pesticide. I said a solution."

"All *solutions* are pesticides."

"There's nothing else?" I asked.

"Lady beetles," Lia said. "Lady beetles eat aphids. As part of the natural life cycle."

"You are comfortable with the homicide of pests by bugs?" Martin said.

Lia glared at him.

"I am joking," Martin said.

"Do they sell ladybugs at pet stores?" Annie asked.

"You can buy them in Switzerland," Lia said.

"So if we buy ladybugs and fish pellets," I tallied, "*then* we'll be even with vegetables. And if we also get goat food . . ." I explained my plan to make cheese, which I believed would bring in as much money as the roses sold by *Les jardiniers suprêmes*.

Martin smiled. "Now we have some good strategies."

"But we are still even with the other team," Lia said.

"That's where our wild card comes in." I pointed to Annie.

She stopped walking. "*I* am the wild card?"

"Your paintings," I said. "Aren't there some glass squares left over?"

"There should be," Annie said. "But I have never *sold* a painting before."

"Have you ever tried?" I asked.

Annie shook her head.

"I would buy one of your paintings," Lia said.

"You don't have money," Annie reminded her.

"If you loaned me some," Lia said.

"People will buy them," I said. "Who else will be selling glass paintings of clouds at a summer festival?"

Annie considered. "I could do some French countrysides as well."

"Whatever you want," I said. "You're the artist."

Annie's face slowly slid into a smile. "I think it could actually work."

"Okay, so we have vegetables, cheese, cherries, paintings, and . . ." I paused dramatically. "*Honey*."

"We are going to win!" Lia squealed.

TWENTY·THREE

The trip to the pet store was a success, which made our journey back more difficult. Lia had the easiest job, carrying the small mesh bag of three hundred ladybugs in one hand and the jar of fish pellets in the other. I had two five-pound bags of goat food, which I carried like two dumbbells. Annie, thankfully, carried the third bag of goat food. Martin, who had the wise idea to buy a cooler so we could keep our cheese plan a secret, enthusiastically led our exhausted group back to the farm, the cooler pressed into his chest.

We returned during peak nap time, so no one saw us trudge our supplies back to the stables and collapse onto our cots. Everyone but Lia, who went to the kitchen to get some ice for the cooler. The instructions on the ladybugs' bag said they should be refrigerated for about six hours before being released, in order to "slow them down." If not, they'd immediately fly away.

We spent the whole afternoon resting alongside the ladybugs. After dinner, Lia removed them from the cooler.

"Do they look slowed down?" I asked as she gently jiggled the bag.

"They look pretty slow. Maybe too slow?"

"Should we heat them back up?" Martin suggested.

"We can give them a few minutes," Lia said. "Besides, we need to water the plants first. The ladybugs won't be attracted to the plants unless there is a reason."

"They find water attractive?" I asked.

"This is a different kind of attraction," Lia said.

"I find water attractive," Annie said quietly as we moved to fill our watering cans.

I poured water slowly over the lettuce and zucchini. Some of the lettuce leaves were lightly torn and starting to sag, signs of the aphid infestation. The zucchini themselves looked healthy, though the vines were beginning to wither. I watched the water gently pool on the leaves until they looked as artfully misted as a grocery-store display.

Lia was lying on her stomach, inspecting our work as we watered, trying to place herself in the mindset of a ladybug. She directed us to add a little more water here and there so that it was spread evenly throughout the garden.

When I finished, I lay down beside her.

"Is it time yet?" I asked.

"Almost. It says the best time to release them is during the 'twilight hour.' Is this twilight?"

"I think so."

"Twilight has multiple definitions," Martin said, joining us on the ground.

"This is twilight," Annie said, lying down on her back. "Look at the stars."

We all rolled onto our backs and marveled at the clarity of the light in the sky.

"Look at the Big Dipper," I said, tracing the most visible constellation with my index finger.

"We call it the Great Wagon," Martin said.

"The Cantonese story is difficult to translate," Annie said.

"You can try," I suggested.

"It is not my specialty," Annie said. "But each star is like the son of the wife of the god of the heavens. Who is also the mother of the god of the heavens? Or sometimes the stars all together are the god of the heavens but also their children? It depends on the night, I think."

"I have little interest in stars," Lia said. "But I memorized all the terms for the groups of insects in English."

"What do you mean?" I asked.

"Like an army of ants."

"I thought it was a swarm of ants," I said.

"A swarm of bees," Lia said. "A colony of beetles. A cluster of dragonflies. A cloud of grasshoppers. A whisper of moths . . ." She trailed off.

"Keep going," Annie said. "This is like a bedtime story."

"A flock of lice," Lia continued.

I scratched at my hair and said, "Maybe skip lice."

"A horde of gnats. A brood of termites. A rainbow of butterflies. A concerto of crickets. A loveliness of ladybugs." She carefully opened the bag, got up, and began gently shaking ladybugs next to the plants. A few immediately flew away, but most clung to where they were released.

I walked to the patch I had watered and knelt down to watch a ladybug lift the body of an aphid into its mouth. As if pulled down a conveyor belt, the aphid disappeared millimeter by millimeter. Aphid consumed, the ladybug plucked another and repeated the process of pushing the pest into its jaws of death. It wasn't very lovely, but if this is what it would take for us to win the contest, I hoped the ladybugs had a big appetite.

TWENTY·FOUR

Wow, I can't believe my luck! Bastille Day is something else. The streets will be packed and the restaurants full. But I know a nice place near me where we could meet. It's called Petit Repas, on 16 Rue de Vaugirard. Just get off at le Jardin du Luxembourg stop, take a right, and you can't miss it. How does 5 p.m. sound?

Can't wait to see you, buddy!

All my best,

Dad

Martin handed back my phone. "I think that he sounds excited," he said.

"I guess a little," I said.

"My father has never used an exclamation point to address me."

"That's just normal email stuff."

"Or called me *buddy*."

"What does he call you?"

Martin thought for a moment. "He just talks in my direction."

"You *really* think he's excited?" I asked again.

"I am not someone who communicates with lies," Martin said. "The only part I think is a little confusing is the ending. *All my best?*"

"That's what everyone says."

"All my best *what?*"

I had never really thought about it before. "Wishes?"

"Why would he give you his best wishes?"

"It's an expression."

"Does your mother say this at the end of her messages?" Martin asked.

I knew the answer but pulled up her last email to show him. "No, she says 'Love.'"

"And 'x-o-x-o'?" he read confusedly.

"Those are hugs and kisses."

Martin took out his flip phone, which I'd rarely seen him use. It didn't get email, but he opened a text message from his father and handed it to me.

"Could you translate?" I asked.

"The message is not of importance. I wanted to show you the ending. The translation would be 'Bye.' With a period. 'Your dad.'"

"Bye. Your dad," I repeated.

"This is the way he always does it," Martin said.

"Even if he misses you?"

"He does not miss me. He is happy that I am pursuing my interests. This is what he is saying in the message."

"My mom said she misses me a lot," I said.

"Did you tell her that you are happily pursuing your interests?"

I thought back to the second day, when I called her minutes after bawling. "Not really."

"Then maybe you should send her a new message," Martin suggested. "After we finish pursuing our interests for the day."

I waited a few days, swept up in the happy pursuit of trying to win the contest. But then I did send a new message to my mom. I told her about my success in convincing Bijou to eat newly bought goat food instead of moist dirt. The pleasure of collecting milk in order to make cheese. How Pierre's mother had an index card that described a goat-cheese-making recipe from the year 1929, and I had followed the steps perfectly.

I described how difficult it was to maintain a garden. How you had to get up early, to always make sure the vegetables were hydrated, to regularly check that the ladybugs you sprinkled throughout the garden were devouring aphids. And I told her about Annie's glass paintings, how she had captured a week's worth of French skies. The way she held up each painting in our stable at night so we could compare it with our experience of the day's sky.

I didn't tell her *why* I was so determined to the win the contest—partly because I knew that's what she would focus on, but also because the outcome had moved from the surface of my thinking. I truly *was* happy pursuing my interests, now that I knew what they were, and everything felt touched by small waves of joy.

This feeling lasted until the week before the summer festival, when we walked into the cherry orchard to discover rows of barren trees. While we had been busy tending to the garden and the goats and the greenhouse, *Les jardiniers suprêmes* had diligently plucked every ripe cherry.

"There's no way they took *all* of them," I said as we walked from one tree to the next.

"I cannot see any that are inside our reach," Martin said, craning his neck to inspect the highest branches. "There are possibly some hidden at the very top."

"I do see some flashes of red," Annie said.

I cupped my hand to try to shade the sun as I looked toward the tallest green shoots of the trees. "But those are, what, forty feet high?" I said. "Even the extension ladder wouldn't come close."

"Which is why we must climb," Martin said dramatically. "Though not me. I have a fear of heights."

"I have a fear of falling," Annie said.

"I have a fear of both," I said.

"I can do it," Lia offered.

"You don't have to," I said. "We could try shaking the trees first."

"Have you seen those videos of the official shaking machines?" Annie asked. "They are very satisfying."

"How do they work?" I asked.

"There are these big umbrellas that spread out underneath the tree, and then this yellow machine puts its, uh, machine hands around the trunk, and"—she mimed shaking with her whole body—"all the cherries scatter onto the umbrellas like little red bouncy balls."

"Should we try it?" I said. "If we all pushed together, we'd be strong. Kind of."

We circled the nearest tree with cherries clinging to the highest branches. All together, we thrust our weight into the tree, dug our heels into the ground, and pressed our palms against the trunk. Despite shoves from every direction, the highest branches remained still. A single cherry fell, but because of the wind, not our strength.

"What's the market price for one cherry?" Martin said.

Lia had already slipped out of her shoes and started stretching. "I can do this, really," she said. "I have climbed bigger trees."

"The branches at the top are so thin," Annie warned.

"It is no problem," Lia said. She walked around the tree, peering upward. "I just need a little boost to start."

As the tallest, Martin offered himself as a human ladder. Lia climbed atop his shoulders and set her hands firmly on the lowest branch.

With the agility of a seasoned tree climber, she quickly made her way up, never flinching or faltering in her path toward the top. It was only when she reached her destination that she started to slow. "I can't . . . reach . . . the cherries," she called.

I could see where her legs were wrapped around a thick branch, but the rest of her body was shaded by green.

"Could you maybe give a *little* shake?" I yelled up. "*Very* little!" I clarified.

"Hold . . . on," she called, moving a few inches forward and readjusting her legs. Along with the sound of rustling branches came a scattering of cherries. Four, and then six, and then ten fell to the grass, and the rustling stopped.

"Beautiful work, Lia!" Annie called.

"We have ten!" Martin called.

"Could you do a few more?" I called up.

Lia slowly inched to the next closest branch and repeated the process, showering us with an even more bountiful batch. Martin quickly sorted them into piles of "sellable" and "questionable" and determined that we had twenty-seven cherries ready to sell.

"This is enough for at least three people," Martin said. "It is not much, but it is something."

"Could we maybe get just a few more?" I asked.

"We do not want to risk it," Annie said.

"Why don't we ask Lia?" I offered.

When we called up to her, Lia said there was one more area with a lot of cherries, but the nearest branch looked a little weak.

"But I can try," she added.

"Be careful!" Annie urged through cupped hands.

Lia cautiously made her way to the most densely cherried section and scooted down the thickest branch. With each scoot, the branch bent further. She moved another few inches down and started to rattle.

A sprinkling of fresh cherries fell. She shook again. But instead of the sound of cherries hitting the ground, there was a sharp crack.

Lia yelped and hugged the branch tightly.

"Hold on!" Annie and I yelled.

There was another crack.

"We will catch you!" Martin shouted.

We could only hear the branch as it snapped, then detached, and then started to fall.

In all the commotion it was difficult to see how she did it, but Lia somehow slid down the trunk of the tree, reaching for a connection. I tried to avoid falling branches while keeping an eye on her, ready to catch her if she came tumbling.

As the branch crashed to the ground, a loud *hummphhh* came from above.

"I . . . am . . . here," Lia choked out. I looked up to find her hanging on with both hands to a sturdy branch in the middle of the tree. She must have fallen about fifteen feet. There was a line of blood running down her knee, and leaves swirled into her hair, but she didn't seem to be otherwise injured.

"You are sure you are okay?" Annie asked.

Lia nodded and, after catching her breath, swung her legs back to the trunk and made her way down within thirty seconds. Annie quickly rushed to hold her in a hug.

"Come on!" She waved Martin and me over. I had never taken part in a group hug, and from the looks of it, neither had Martin, but we extended our arms and formed a circle around Lia.

"Our hero," Annie said.

When we counted the cherries brought down by the crash, we had a full batch of fifty-eight. Certainly not as many as Wilder's crew had collected, but enough to keep us in the contest.

TWENTY·FIVE

With just three days remaining until the summer festival, we had stockpiled an impressive collection of items for sale. Annie's glass paintings—ten in total—were carefully wrapped in rags and laid in a stack underneath her cot. My four logs of goat cheese were in the cooler beneath my cot, "aging" to perfection (I hoped). Our basket of cherries was likewise kept cool beneath Lia's cot to preserve their freshness. All that remained was to harvest the vegetables.

Since releasing the ladybugs, almost all the aphids had fled or been gruesomely consumed. There was no way to know if the fish pellets had truly enriched the soil, but to my eye the vegetables looked as healthy as ever. Everything seemed to be going our way, until the fates intervened.

I had just fallen into a deep midday rest in the barn when I felt the first raindrop plop onto my forehead. I opened my eyes just in time to get another drop right in the pupil. When I'd regained full consciousness, I realized that we had bigger problems than a leak in the roof. Outside, a sweeping rainstorm was picking up in intensity.

Rain splashed down through the open door and started to spread across the dirt floor. Despite the sound of rain crashing against the barn, everyone else was still asleep.

Following the path of water on the floor, I rushed over to Annie's cot, kneeling to collect her paintings before the water hit them. With the full stack in my arms, I tried waking her.

Nothing.

I leaned down and carefully nudged with my shoulder.

She immediately shot up. "It's here," she said.

"What?"

"I was dreaming," Annie said. "Am I awake?"

"Yes! I need your help." I set the paintings into her arms.

"Are they not good enough?" she asked, still dazed.

"They're beautiful," I said hurriedly. "But it's, I mean, look—" I pointed to the window.

Annie looked delighted. "I have been waiting all summer

for a French rain. This is a bit intense, though."

"Too intense," I said. "I'm worried about the vegetables drowning. Can you help wake up Martin and Lia?"

"Who said my name?" Martin called from his cot. Before I could answer, he noticed the torrential downpour and whipping winds and sprang for his shoes. "Where could we find a plastic covering? I don't know the English. Like a blanket for the vegetables."

"A tarp?" I asked.

"As I said, I don't know the English." His shoes on, Martin rose from his cot with purpose.

"There are plastic blankets in the greenhouse," Annie said.

"Then let's go!" I yelled, waking Lia.

"Go . . ." she repeated.

"We are saving the garden," Annie informed her.

"Rain is good . . . for . . . lettuce," Lia said sleepily.

"Light rain is good," Martin said. "Not pelting rain."

Lia agreed and pulled on her shoes.

Mud speckled my legs and rain drenched my shirt as I led the charge into the greenhouse. Annie had already returned almost every square of glass to its rightful place, so there were just a few square-shaped holes where water shot through with the pressure of a showerhead. Crumpled in a corner was a single blue tarp.

"Didn't you say blan-*kets*?" I said to Annie, stressing the *s*.

"There were at least five yesterday," Annie said.

"The French strike again." Martin groaned.

"*Hoooowwwww?*" I yelled with more intensity than I had intended.

Everyone seemed taken aback by my howl.

Eventually Martin asked, "Are . . . you . . . all right?"

"I'm sorry," I responded quickly. "I just—I don't understand how they keep doing things before us. It doesn't seem fair."

"They have not done anything *un*fair," Martin said.

"You know what I mean," I said. "They got the better garden, the better rooms, they're closer to the greenhouse, they're closer to the cherries. And they're going to win the day in Paris, which they don't even need. They're *from* Paris."

"Michel is from Saint-Tropez," Lia corrected.

"Which is even more beautiful than Paris!" I said. "But that's not the point."

The rain continued to pour as everyone waited for me to get to the point.

"The point is I *need* to win. I already promised someone

I would meet them in Paris on Bastille Day, and it's . . . really important."

"Like a girlfriend or something?" Lia asked.

"I don't have a girlfriend," I said.

"A boyfriend?" Annie asked.

"It's not someone like that," I said. "It's my father." What was meant to be the big reveal came out more like a whisper.

"Oh, that's nice!" Lia immediately perked up. "I'm missing my poppa, too. I wish he would come to Paris."

"He lives there," I said.

"And you've never been?" Annie said.

"I haven't seen him since I was three," I said slowly.

There was a surprised silence. A whirring of rain.

Then Martin put his right hand on my shoulder and gently squeezed. "You will get the chance to see him again," he said.

Annie collected the tarp as Lia gave me a hug, then turned to the others. "Let's save the garden. For Rylan."

A cheer rose around me, and I joined in. Then we took off in a sprint toward the garden.

We were surprised by what we found. The trenches were collecting most of the rainwater, so despite the intensity of the downpour, there didn't seem to be too much damage. Martin used a pair of gardening shears to cut the tarp into three smaller sections, which we draped over the tomatoes, asparagus, and zucchini. I dug around to find rocks heavy enough to hold the tarp's edges down against the harsh winds, and Lia made sure that I wasn't smashing any of the writhing earthworms in the process.

Compared with the professionally tarped garden of *Les jardiniers suprêmes*, who somehow found both rope and stakes to seal every inch of their *schrebergarten* from the rain, ours looked pretty ramshackle. Part of me wanted to rip up their stakes, steal their tarps, and let their vegetables drown, but I'd developed too much respect for gardening to ruin their efforts.

We returned to the stables drenched but giddy with the feeling that we truly had saved the garden. To prevent any of our cots from getting soaked, we positioned them in the center of the stable, forming a diamond. After the giddiness passed, the exhaustion of sprinting through the rain hit us.

"It is even more like a sleepover than usual," Lia said.

"I'm not really tired, though," Annie said. "Going-to-sleep tired, I mean."

"I am going to sleep," Martin said.

"You can't be the first person who falls asleep at a sleepover," I said. "It's like a rule."

"I did not know this," Martin said. "I have never been to a sleepover."

"Awww," Annie and Lia cooed, while I said, "Really?"

"What do you do if you do not sleep?" he asked.

"Play video games, eat pizza," I said.

"Not at my sleepovers," Lia said. "We gossip at great length and then—"

"Inspect insects," I said.

Lia laughed. "If it is at my home."

"Typically, we make B-B-Q," Annie said. "And tell scary stories."

Lia nearly jumped off her cot in excitement. "I love scary stories! Swiss stories are the scariest."

Martin raised his index finger. "I believe that German stories are the scariest."

"You clearly have not heard Chinese ghost stories," Annie said.

For the rest of the afternoon, we took turns sharing the scariest stories we could remember. So enraptured did we become in the tales of ghosts and monsters and witches, we didn't even notice when the rain stopped.

TWENTY·SIX

Our vegetables were minimally damaged by the storm. The tomatoes had to be harvested a day earlier than Martin had planned, and a few of the zucchini became too waterlogged to sell, but the rest had survived.

With only a day until the festival, the last thing I had to do was harvest the honey. Pierre met me at the table just as I was finishing the previous day's edition of *Le Monde*. Coincidentally, it featured an article about bees, or at least an article featuring a picture of an unhappy-looking beekeeper.

Pierre was already outfitted in his beekeeper suit, his hands filled with tools.

"Ah, you have read it," he said, carefully laying our equipment on the table.

"Parts of it," I said. "The beekeeper is sad?"

"Sad, yes." He draped my suit over an empty chair before sitting down. "But a better word is *somber*. He is sad now but also for the future."

"Because the bees are dying?" I guessed.

"Of course, yes, but for him it is more about the honey." Pierre drew the newspaper toward him to translate. "In the past, every bee would produce one small spoon of honey in its life. You could expect about the same amount from each bee. Now most of the bees make a much smaller spoon. Altogether, there is much less honey in the world."

"Now *I'm* sad," I said.

"Not for long." Pierre closed the newspaper. "Because this is the trend for all bees. But not the trend for good bees."

I suited up, put on the gloves, grabbed the smoker, and followed Pierre to the secret location where the good bees had hopefully produced their spoons of honey over the past twenty-eight days. The buzzing box was in the thicket of woods between the gardens and the stable, resting at the trunk of a twisted tree. Though my first encounter with the bees had gone relatively well, I was still spiking with nerves as we approached.

"We must be careful to keep the queen inside," Pierre explained. "This will only be a *scrape* of honey. More will be coming in a month or so. Unless the queen escapes."

"How do we know which one is the queen?" I asked.

"You will know. She is the largest." Pierre knelt down. "Ready for the smoke?"

I squeezed the smoker bag and released a light puff.

Pierre lifted the top lid, and a cluster of bees flew out. "Come closer," he urged. "Get a smoke ready. A big smoke, but slow, gentle."

I moved forward and positioned my hand on the smoke bag. Pierre signaled to me like a conductor. As he lifted out a rectangular slab of wood, I let out a big, not very gentle plume of smoke. Pierre coughed and ducked his head as the bees darted toward me. I felt them pelting every inch of my suit, and I stumbled backward, trying not to fall. I instinctively grabbed hold of the smoke bag and let out another huge puff, this one helping to disperse the bees, who scattered to different trees.

"Sorry," I said as I made my way back to Pierre.

"It is okay," he said. "I did not see the queen in their attack on you. But I also do not see much honey." He showed me the slab, properly called the *frame*, and explained how it was meant to be covered in honeycomb, beneath which we would find pure, delicious honey. Unfortunately, the frame was mostly *un*covered by honeycomb, except a few patches at the corners. Pierre scraped these bits of honeycomb into a glass jar using a comblike tool.

"There are more frames, though, right?" I said, peering into the box.

"There are four others, but the first is typically a sign."

My face darkened beneath the bee veil.

"But we never know." Pierre placed the first frame back in the box. "Prepare the smoke."

I couldn't see his face behind his veil, but I knew he had just winked.

I laid down a consistent mist of smoke while Pierre pulled out the frames and scraped what he could find. But he did not find very much. After clearing every available millimeter of honeycomb, barely a third of the glass jar was filled.

"I guess the article was right," I said as we sat a few feet from the box, waiting for the angered bees to return to their queen.

"It is too early to say. The honey season lasts for two months more." Pierre tilted the jar to catch the light. "It is still beautiful, no?"

"Yes, but—"

"No *but*," Pierre said. "Look." He slowly spun the jar in the sunlight. The honeycomb shone like gold.

"It's beautiful," I said honestly. But not too beautiful

to divert my original thought. "*However*, this is what, two inches of honey?"

"Maybe. A little less, perhaps. I am not good with inches." Pierre passed me the jar and maneuvered beneath his beekeeper suit to produce a cigarette and lighter.

"Who's going to buy two inches of honey?" I said.

"I would buy it," Pierre said.

"Are you going to?"

"I am remaining outside of the contest. No purchases for either side." He took a drag of his cigarette. "But if it was me, with this little bit of honey, I would mix it with some ice cream."

"I can use the Donvier maker?" I asked eagerly.

"Why not?" Pierre shrugged. "Hot day tomorrow."

"I thought you weren't taking sides," I said.

"I have no favorites, but I do understand why you want to win." Pierre looked at me as if he knew a secret.

"Did my mom tell you?" I asked.

"No," Pierre said. "But you did. On the first night."

I thought back to the Tarot reading. "You *actually* read my mind?"

"I *felt* it." He took a drag on his cigarette as I pondered his abilities. "Also, a friend of your mother sent me an email message"

I pushed Pierre's shoulder. "Come *onnnn*."

"Careful, careful." He laughed, trying not to set his bee-keeper suit on fire.

"So you've known the whole time?" I asked.

"I know what was shared with me," Pierre said. "And I know how important this contest is for you."

"But you're not going to help me win."

"It is up to the fates to decide," he said, spreading his hands skyward.

"Yeah, yeah," I said.

"I remember giving a little hint about some ice cream, though."

I picked up the jar of honeycomb. "Thank you."

"Thank the bees," Pierre said.

I stood up and lowered my bee veil. "*Thank you, bees*," I whispered as I fit the lid back on the box.

TWENTY·SEVEN

On the morning of the festival I awoke even earlier than usual. The sun wasn't even up, but a combination of nerves, excitement, and the desire to win kept me from falling back asleep.

The cheese was ready, kept cool under my cot, waiting to be sliced, but I needed some fresh milk to make ice cream. The grass was still damp as I headed toward the wild zone.

For the first time in two weeks I saw *Les jardiniers suprêmes* at work in the rose garden. Wilder was on flashlight duty, illuminating a bed of pink roses. Michel was making precise cuts and placing the sellable roses in a bucket.

I thought I'd be able to snoop undetected, but Wilder heard my footsteps and shined his flashlight on my face.

"A spy!" he hooted.

"Come on." I shielded my eyes from the blinding light. "I'm not spying. I know you're cutting roses."

"But you don't know how many," Wilder said, keeping the light on me as if I were a criminal under investigation.

"It doesn't matter," I said. "You could sell a hundred roses and you'll still lose."

A chorus of French jeers came from the dark. I stepped out of the spotlight and walked away.

"We'll see!" Wilder called after me.

In truth, the number of roses they had prepared to sell was concerning. But I tried not to think about that, instead tabulating everything we would need.

Yesterday Pierre had assigned both groups a table and given us cardboard to make a sign. We decided to call ourselves Pierre's Protégés, and, around our title, Annie had painted emoji-style symbols of what we had for sale: tomatoes, lettuce, zucchini, asparagus, cheese, paintings, and ice cream. The vegetables were already placed in woven baskets and washed to give off that "buy me" glimmer. The frozen metal interior of the Donvier ice cream maker lay waiting inside the freezer.

The sun was starting to rise, spreading a golden band of light across the wild zone. If everything went according to plan, this would be my last day with Bijou.

She seemed to sense it, immediately running over, nestling against my legs, and cleaning mud from the bottoms of my shoes. I sat cross-legged in the grass, and she settled down next to me as we watched the sun continue to rise.

"I will miss you, Bijou," I said.

She gazed back at me with big brown eyes, and it seemed like she understood.

After collecting the milk, I waved goodbye to the rest of the goats, locked the gate, and carried the pail back to the stable.

Everyone else was awake and had set out our supplies neatly on the cots. On mine was a mixing bowl and spoon, a bottle of vanilla, a jar of honey, and a handful of cherries.

I raised the pail. "And here's the final ingredient."

They helped me measure the proportions, and then I mixed everything together.

"Do we have bowls and spoons?" I asked Martin.

"Pierre said people would keep them if we used his real bowls and spoons," Martin said. "But we can stop somewhere along the way to buy some cheap ones."

"Then we'd better get going," I said. I turned the ice cream crank a final time, removed it, and put the entire

Donvier kit into the cooler.

"We're ready!" Annie and Lia both called.

We carried our wares to the field in front of the castle, where Pierre had pulled up in a rusted red truck.

"I like your sign," he called.

"I like your truck," Annie called back.

"It is from my neighbor," Pierre said. "He just left with the other group."

"They're already *there*?" I gasped.

"Don't worry," Pierre said. "We will soon be there."

He laid down some blankets and helped us drag the table into the back of the truck. There was one seat next to him, but we all decided to ride in the back. Pierre cranked the old engine and sped down the dirt road out of the château.

TWENTY·EIGHT

Festival d'été de Dreux was painted on a banner that hung at the entrance of a large field. It was nine a.m. and already turning out to be a perfect summer day. The festival opened to the public in an hour, and every minute a new caravan of vendors pulled up.

There were no laws about who sold what or where, so everyone jostled to find the best spot. Two long rows of tables had developed, and at the end of the aisle between the rows was a wooden stage, where a violinist played a slow waltz.

An aroma of freshly baked bread filled the air as Martin and I carried our table down the center aisle. We stopped at the sound of a mocking *"Bonjjoouuurrrr"* from a familiar voice.

Les jardiniers suprêmes, whose sign looked amateurish compared to ours, had found a prime position in the center of the first row. Despite their lackluster signage, the rest of their table display was perfect. Their tomatoes looked shinier and redder than ours, their lettuce crisper. Their artichokes were arranged in a basket like a still-life painting, and their cherries glittered like gemstones. Michel was still arranging their bucket of roses, but even without them, their stand would be tough to beat.

"Want to be our first customer?" Wilder asked as he unzipped their money pouch.

"No thank you," Martin said flatly.

I said, "Good luck" in as unfriendly a voice as I could.

We found an empty spot close to the stage. Martin propped open our table and agreed to guard it while I went back to the truck to help Lia and Annie haul our goods.

I took careful notice of what else was for sale, thankful that we weren't in competition with everyone. Some farmers had multiple tables pushed together, their bounty overflowing. Others were selling handmade tie-dye shirts and puzzle books. One was making artisanal caramel candy and giving out free samples.

The first table in our row was entirely devoted to cheeses, which looked *much* better than my goat-cheese logs. But having such an appetizing table nearby could play to our advantage. If they sold out early, cheese buyers would need to search for another stand. Even better, I didn't see anyone selling ice cream.

Though Pierre said he would remain a neutral participant throughout the day, he did help us carry supplies from the truck. He had warned us that he was not popular among most of the real farmers, who found him to be a foolish dilettante, but several people seemed happy to see him.

"I am going to check with the others," Pierre said once he set our baskets of vegetables down. "And then disappear for a while."

"You're leaving?" I asked.

"I will be around but out of sight. Good luck." He smiled and turned, greeting the farmers next to us in jubilant French.

We carefully arranged our offerings. Annie stood in the center aisle directing us on the proper angles of presentation. She gave the final thumbs-up just seconds before the announcement that the festival was now open to the public.

We huddled together like an American football team. "Everyone put their hands in the center," I directed.

Martin placed his hand in the center. "European football teams also do this," he clarified.

Lia added her hand. "And my volleyball team."

Annie excitedly thrust her hand forward. "I have never done this."

I said, "On three, we're going to shout *Protégés*."

"*Un!*"

"*Deux!*"

"*Trois!*"

"*Protégés!*"

After receiving strange looks from the other sellers, we anxiously took our spots behind the table. Onstage, the violinist was joined by a small band, and the aisles filled with potential customers.

Potential customers who were not that interested in what we had for sale. We did sell a few zucchini and a tomato and a handful of asparagus to a polite older couple who wanted to practice their English, but our vegetables could not compete with those from professional farmers. The cheese remained untouched, everyone who stopped by already carrying a block from the first table. And Annie's paintings didn't merit more than a smile.

At noon, I volunteered to scout our competition. Trying

my best to mix into the crowd, I peered at *Les jardiniers suprêmes'* table from a distance. Their vegetables had sold a little better than ours, though just barely. But their roses were almost sold out.

I approached a woman carrying a rose and, in my best French, asked, "How much money—the flower is what?"

The woman looked bewildered but held up five fingers.

"*Cinq euros?*" I asked.

The woman nodded and dashed away, looking over her shoulder to make sure I wasn't following her.

I knew they had at least twenty roses in their bucket, and therefore an enormous lead above our nine euros. Our only hope was to start selling the paintings and the ice cream.

By now there was a small crowd gathered around the stage, and. I had to squeeze past to make it back to our table.

"How does it look?" Martin asked.

"Bad. Really bad. But I have an idea." I leaned down and lifted the ice cream maker out of the cooler, explaining my plan as I scooped cherry ice cream into three bowls.

"If we could just get one person to taste it," I said, "we'd have them lining up."

"Should we give one away for free?" Lia suggested.

"You're a genius," I said.

Lia blushed.

I stuck a spoon into a bowl of ice cream and passed it to her. "Find someone with lots of friends."

She saluted and ducked into the crowd.

TWENTY·NINE

Lia returned with a group of college students who looked like they had been partying much longer than the three hours that the festival had been open. Which was good, because it meant they were in the mood to buy a lot of ice cream.

"Form a line," Lia told them in French.

They formed a loose circle around her. While they laughed, pushed one another, and hollered things I didn't understand, Lia gave a sales pitch for Annie's paintings.

She lifted a glass painting into the air and encouraged them to look at the painted cloud while the real clouds moved behind it. The group stopped jostling one another and stared, as if they were examining an optical illusion.

"*Tripppp-pppyyyyy*," one of them said in English.

"It is how much?" another asked.

"It is ten for—" Annie started.

Lia interrupted. "*Fifteen* euros. Each."

He took out a twenty-euro bill and placed it on the table. I handed him his ice cream, and Annie handed him a glass painting wrapped in newspaper. His five friends each bought a bowl of ice cream, and one added a painting to his order.

"Now the others will come," Lia said.

"How do you know?" Martin asked.

"It is not easy to collect insects," Lia said. "I have learned some tricks about attracting a crowd."

Like ants drawn to a cookie crumb, our table was soon swarmed. We sold out of the first batch of ice cream within the hour. Although we hadn't sold more vegetables, only one cheese log and four glass paintings remained.

We had to momentarily shoo customers away as I made more ice cream. But being close to the stage now played to our advantage as the turned-away customers stayed nearby to enjoy the band.

Our first customer had made it to the front of the audience and was twirling his glass painting in the air as the band played. A few people behind him were equally transfixed by the movement of clouds through the glass. Before the second batch of ice cream was fully mixed, Annie had sold two more paintings.

By the end of the band's set, we had a full line of customers. I knew this was our last chance—it was clear that no more lettuce or asparagus would sell to this crowd of partyers—so I made the ice cream scoops smaller, trying to stretch what remained.

After we sold out of ice cream and paintings, we spent the last hour dancing with the remaining vegetables in our hands, trying to lure the crowd. We sold only one tomato as a result, but every euro counted.

With five minutes remaining, Pierre casually weaved his way through the crowd.

"Looking good," he said appraisingly at our mostly bare table.

"How does the other group look?" I asked.

He put his finger to his lips. "It is a secret. Soon you will find out."

He slipped back into the audience to enjoy the final performance. Everyone who had taken the stage throughout the day returned for a rendition of "La Marseillaise," the French national anthem. The crowd swayed and sang along until the final bow. Then the festival organizers waved everyone away, and there was a slow migration toward the exit.

Once the field cleared, I could finally see what remained on *Les jardiniers suprêmes'* table: almost nothing. The roses were gone, and so were the lettuce and tomatoes. All that was left were a few artichokes.

They likewise surveyed the vegetables remaining on our table and smiled tauntingly.

Pierre stood between the tables and waved us over to join him. "Ready for the count?"

Emile thrust their money pouch forward, and Pierre kept track aloud, deliberately raising each bill and coin so we could verify his tabulation.

"One hundred and eighty-five euros," Pierre called.

Les jardiniers suprêmes turned the number into a sing-song chant and began to dance.

"Beat that," Wilder spat our way.

While I had lost track at the end, I knew we had to be close. Martin handed our money pouch to Pierre, and he repeated the counting process.

"One hundred and seventy. One hundred and seventy-five. One hundred and eighty. One hundred and eighty-five." Pierre stuck his hand back into the pouch and paused. His eyes scanned everyone but seemed to hold on mine. He lifted a ten-euro bill out of the pouch. "One . . . hundred . . . ninety-five!"

Lia tackled me, and I landed on my knees. I think she meant to hug me, but I wasn't ready for it. She helped lift me up, and we all jumped around in a circle, not paying attention to the additional twenty euros that Pierre had pulled from our pouch.

Les jardiniers suprêmes were in disbelief, muttering among themselves as they stomped off in defeat.

"We will leave at noon," Pierre told us. "I think you will enjoy Bastille Day very much."

THIRTY

Before we left Château de Beaulieu for the final time, I went down the line giving *faire la bise* to Emile, Simone, and Michel, agreeing that it was such a pleasure to meet them, though I didn't mean it and neither did they. I didn't kiss Wilder's cheeks but shook his hand politely, even though I would see him again.

The car buzzed with lively conversation on the way to the train station, but I was having difficulty following it. I had emailed my father early that morning to tell him that I would be at the café at five o'clock. I'd deliberately sent it a full two hours before we'd be leaving, so I'd have time to check his response. By the time we left, he hadn't responded.

I checked again at the train station, and there was still nothing. A queasy feeling started to rise in my stomach. I thought about sending another message. Maybe mine had fallen too far down in his inbox. But there wasn't time before the train doors opened.

Inside, nearly every seat was filled with people festively dressed in blue, white, and red. Some had celebratory signs next to their seats, and many families were outlining their plans for when they arrived in Paris. I pressed my way through to find an empty seat, and Martin squeezed in next to me. He was not festively dressed, but was practicing his French by shouting along with a group, trying to start a chant.

He nudged me to join in, but I couldn't get much volume into my voice.

"Are you still feeling nervous?" Martin shouted through the noise.

"Kind of!" I yelled back. "I mean, yes. Very."

"There is nothing to be nervous about."

"That's not very helpful."

"I'm sorry!" Martin said with as much compassion as you can put into a shout.

"It's okay!" I shouted back.

Another round of chanting started. This time, Martin didn't join in.

When it stopped, he said, "Would it be helpful to do a rehearsal?"

"A what?"

"A practice of what you will say."

"*Here?*" I hollered.

"No one is listening to us."

I hadn't thought of what I was going to say. I was hoping my father would do most of the talking, would explain things to me in a way that made sense. Why he left, why he waited so long to write me, why he had never called. But I wasn't necessarily going to ask these questions.

I nodded to Martin, and he stood a little taller, repositioning himself to take on the role of my father. "You have grown!" he shouted.

"He won't say that!"

"It is what fathers say!"

"But I'm short!"

"But you *have* grown!"

"Fine." I looked at Martin, trying to imagine my father's face. "You've grown, too!"

"I am big now, yes!"

"Come on." I laughed.

"What's for dinner?!" Martin yelled.

"You picked the restaurant!"

"It is my favorite! That is why I invited you here!"

"To eat?"

"And meet! And talk!" Martin raised his eyebrows, prodding me to continue.

"Why?" I said softly.

"What?"

"Why?!" I yelled. "Why now?!"

"Because I miss you!"

"You don't know me!"

"I want to know you!"

"No you don't!"

"I am here."

"But why?"

"I told you."

"I don't believe you!"

Martin blinked. He didn't know what to say, and he dropped out of character. "You really think you will say those things to your father?"

"Probably not."

THIRTY·ONE

Before we arrived in Paris, Pierre warned us that the streets would be crowded and told us to always keep him in sight. Until the train stopped, I thought he was exaggerating. I could barely move, my body pushed from every side as I tried to follow Pierre out of the station. Miniature French flags were thrown around like confetti, and I was nearly punched in the eye as someone tried to grab one next to my face.

"This is so exciiittiinnngggg!" Lia yelled from below. She was a foot shorter than most of the subway crowd and was being pinballed around, doing her best to hold on to Annie's hand.

"Does the screaming stop at some point?" Annie tried to ask Pierre, but he couldn't hear her. The official parade was ending, but the streets were still thronged with people collecting white flower blossoms that dropped from the sky like parachutes. The people who weren't picking up flowers were busy making out. It was like the moment the ball drops on New Year's Eve, but all day long.

Pierre led us through the crowds to the door of the place where I would meet my father, Petit Repas, a large café with tables outside and two floors inside. We arrived five minutes early, and all the outside tables were full. I scanned the faces of everyone enjoying an afternoon drink.

"Anyone familiar?" Pierre asked me.

I shook my head.

He called over one of the waiters and whispered several long sentences into his ear.

The waiter led me to an empty table in the center of the café, in direct sight of the entrance. Annie, Lia, and Martin stayed outside, but Pierre came with me and sat down.

"I told the waiter to bring you whatever you want," Pierre said. "We're going to be right across there." He pointed to another café across the street. "If there is any . . . trouble, you can just wave to me. Okay?"

My right leg was trembling a little under the table, my body refusing to keep cool. "Okay," I said. "I mean, thank you."

"Take a deep breath." As he did on the first morning on the farm, Pierre demonstrated how to breathe deeply.

I slowly breathed in and then out. My leg steadied, and my face must have brightened, because Pierre's face softened into a smile.

"That is better," he said. "You have nothing to worry about." He rose from his chair. "You can join us later for the fireworks. We'll be at le Jardin du Luxembourg." With that, he turned and left.

The waiter brought me a glass of water and a basket of bread with butter. I ate the first slice slowly, keeping my eyes on the entrance. It was now five o'clock, and I knew the next person that walked through the door would be my father.

Except it wasn't. It was a couple, laughing, arm in arm, coming to join their friends.

I spread butter across the second slice of bread and started pulling it apart into small pieces. I told myself that after I ate the first piece, he would walk through the door.

I popped the first bread ball into my mouth.

A woman came through the front door.

I ate another.

A few seconds later, an elderly man hobbled in.

I checked my phone: 5:10.

I watched a family a few tables away order their food. The waiter turned from the table and started walking toward me.

"Would you like anything to eat?" He passed me a menu.

"Oh no. I'm waiting for someone."

The waiter looked displeased and turned away.

I looked at my phone again: 5:15.

I started to wonder if I had the time wrong, or the day, even though I knew I didn't. Or maybe it was a different Petit Repas.

I called the waiter over and asked, "Is this Petit Repas?"

He stared at me, pointed to the name on the menu, and read very slowly, as if I didn't know how, "*Petit. Repas.*"

"Is there maybe *another* Petit Repas?"

"We are the one and only in Paris."

"Thank you," I said.

"Still waiting for someone?" the waiter asked.

"Yes. I'll have a little more water while I'm waiting, please." I tried to smile.

The waiter nodded and left.

I checked my phone again: 5:25.

I started to worry that he got in a car accident but consoled myself by remembering that he would probably come by train. Maybe that was the problem. The train was late. The crowds had gotten larger. He was just a few miles away, still waiting outside the train.

The waiter brought the water. I took a sip, and then another. I decided to use the bathroom and took it as an opportunity to get a better survey of the restaurant, to make sure that I hadn't missed anyone.

I poked my head outside and scanned the tables. No one looked familiar. I started to wonder if I would even recognize my father if I saw him. Or if he would recognize me. I realized that I had never sent a picture of what I looked like now.

I returned to my table and suddenly felt very hot. I checked my phone again: 5:45. I decided I would give him ten more minutes.

Ten minutes came and passed, but I couldn't bring myself to leave. I started to feel a sense of rising desperation. The family who had ordered was now eating contentedly, and I forced myself to look away from them.

I started to think about what I would say to everyone. *How was it?* Martin would ask.

Imagining my response, I started to cry.

Before anyone could see the tears streaming down my face, I threw a few euros on the table and rushed out of the restaurant. My vision was blurry and the streets were packed, but I pushed ahead, trying to find somewhere I could be alone.

Behind me, someone grabbed my shoulder. I turned: it was Pierre. I pressed my face into his torso and allowed myself to sob.

"It's okay," he said.

"He didn't come," I said into his chest.

"I know."

We were stopped in the middle of a busy sidewalk, and someone thudded into us.

"Let's keep going," Pierre said.

I lifted my head, wiping the tears with the back of my hand, and we started to walk side by side down the block and into le Jardin du Luxembourg. It was just as packed as the streets, filled with families and friends and picnics.

"I know a secret spot," Pierre said.

He led me behind a stage where a marionette show was being performed. We sat on an empty bench facing the back side of the kneeling performers.

"What's the show?" I asked.

"It is not important," Pierre said. "How are you feeling?"

I took a deep breath. "I don't want to talk about it."

"Tell me how you are feeling," he repeated.

"I'm feeling like . . . I feel like—" I started to tear up again. "Why didn't he come?"

"It is who he is," Pierre said.

"What do you mean?"

"He is someone who does not show up."

"But why?"

"I don't know why. Some people are like this."

"But he lied about it. He said he was so excited to see me."

"It is not about you. He would lie to anyone who is his son."

"I don't know if that's true."

"It is true. If he knew who his son truly was, he would be here," Pierre said. "He would not miss the chance."

I wanted to smile, but instead came tears. Pierre laid his hand on my shoulder.

The garden erupted in applause as the marionette show ended. Everyone in the audience gave a standing ovation.

As the noise settled and the performers started to pack up, I asked, "What do I do now?"

Pierre paused. "Do you want to hear a story?"

"Is this story going to make sense?" I asked.

He laughed. "I hope so. It is not my story, but from the Buddha. Do you know him?"

"I've heard of him."

"This is many years ago. The Buddha, he is talking with one of his students and he asks, 'Do you think it hurts when a person is struck with an arrow?'

"'Yes, of course,' the student says.

"Then the Buddha says, 'And do you think it hurts more if the same person is then struck with a second arrow?'

"'Of course, yes, it is even more painful,' the student says.

"So the Buddha says, 'Life is the first arrow. There is no way to stop it from piercing you. But the second arrow, that is your reaction to the first.'" Pierre raised his finger with a flourish. "*You* decide if you want to keep poking yourself with the second arrow. You understand?"

"I think so," I said. "But the first arrow hurts so much."

"I know," Pierre said. He gestured toward the people in the crowded park. "Each of these people has been struck at some time in their life. Some many times. But look at them now."

I looked around at everyone laughing, laying out blankets on the grass, getting ready for the fireworks. A lone man next to a bush was doing tai chi. And Annie, Lia, and Martin, who were rushing toward us.

"We thought we had lost you!" Martin said.

"You have found us," Pierre said.

"How was it?" Martin asked.

"I'll tell you later," I said, and turned to Pierre. "Could I borrow your phone?"

"Of course." He handed it over.

I walked a few yards away and dialed Mom's number. It rang a few times but then went to voice mail. I hadn't thought about what I was going to say but decided to leave a message anyway.

"Hi, Mom, it's me, Rylan. I was supposed to meet up with my . . . I had planned to have dinner with . . . I can tell you about it later. I'm walking in a park right now, in Paris, and everyone is lying on blankets, looking up at the sky. It's just starting to get dark. And I wanted to tell you that . . . I love you. I'm . . . thank you."

I walked back to the bench.

"The last protégé has returned," Pierre said. "The show should start soon."

Right on cue came the first crack of the fireworks. Rainbow sparks filled the sky. My friends and I nestled together in the center of the bench, leaving Pierre on his own at the end. I looked over at him, the light from the fireworks reflected across his face.

"It is beautiful, no?" he said.

"Yes," I said. "It's very beautiful."

THIRTY-TWO

Pierre would not let us leave France without having a proper breakfast at his favorite café in Paris. He had called ahead to reserve an outdoor table for us, which was not something the café allowed, but they made an exception for Pierre.

"No menus," he told the waiter. "*On va prend un grand petit déjeuner. Comme d'habitude. Merci.*"

The waiter nodded.

"Who can do the translation?" Pierre asked.

"We are something a big little breakfast. With something," I tried.

"We desire a great breakfast. Like always," Annie said.

"We are going to have a large breakfast. It is our custom," Martin offered.

"Precisely translated it means 'We will take a big breakfast. As always,'" Lia corrected.

Pierre smiled. "When did everyone become so fluent?"

"In the stable," Lia said. "I conducted language lessons."

"Using my French vocabularies textbook," Martin added.

Pierre brought his hands together. "Now you see the wisdom of the fates."

I thought back to the first day on the farm, when I'd raised my leaf in the air. The wind could have pushed me toward thirty days with Wilder. Thirty days with the French students, lounging around, only occasionally working. That's what I thought I wanted.

But the fates knew better. They pushed me away from Wilder. Toward people who wanted to know me. Toward people I wanted to know.

The waiter set down my big breakfast: two flaky croissants with Charentes-Poitou butter, warm goat cheese on Poilâne bread, vanilla yogurt, and a glass of freshly squeezed orange juice.

We ate slowly and with delight, sharing our favorite memories from the summer.

When we finished, Pierre lifted a leather carrying case from underneath his chair. "I would not be a proper host without leaving you each with a gift."

He handed Lia an illustration of a praying mantis.

"A *Mantis religiosa*!" Lia leaped out of her seat to give Pierre a hug. "How did you know I keep a mantis as a pet?"

"I did not know," Pierre said. "A mantis makes a good pet?"

"The best pet."

"You can play with it?"

"No. I watch her. Observe her behavior. Take notes."

"I am happy you like it," Pierre said while fishing in his bag for the next gift. He brought out a wooden paintbrush with a small black tip.

"It is beautiful," Annie said.

"It was left behind by my former wife," Pierre explained.

"You never told us you were married," I said.

"It was many years ago. She was an artist. Is an artist."

"Why did you get a divorce?" Martin asked.

"It is complicated," Pierre said. "We are still friends, but she will not touch her old tools. So, it is for you." He handed it to Annie and returned to his bag of gifts.

"For my young farming friend." He pulled out a thin book titled *Révolution de l'agriculture biologique* and gave it to Martin.

"I can keep practicing my French vocabularies," Martin said, then thanked him.

"And your farming technique," Pierre said. "You have a bright future."

Martin beamed.

"Last, but not the least." Pierre set down a Tarot card in front of me. A king holding a staff sat on a throne, looking to his right. "Do you remember?"

Of course I remembered. It was the last card of my Tarot reading. The one that led me to write to my father. A month ago, I thought he was the king looking away from me, waiting for me to make a connection. But now I know that wasn't true.

Pierre tapped the card with his fingertip. "It is you. The King of Wands. Intelligent. Eager to learn. And now charged with experience. The Tarot, like the fates, does not lie."

I didn't feel like a king, but I did feel charged with new experiences, and I wished I didn't have to leave. But I had no choice. I had to catch a train to meet Serena and Wilder.

Annie, Lia, and Martin were all flying back home in a few hours. Alongside Pierre, they walked me to my train.

"I'm not good at saying goodbye," I warned them, wanting to say some meaningful thank-you, but not knowing how.

"You do not need to say goodbye," Pierre said. "In French we say *au revoir*. It means 'Until we see each other again.'"

I smiled. "Thank you, and *au revoir*."

I boarded the train and found a seat next to the window. My friends were all laughing and waving, and I waved back from behind the glass. I turned and watched them grow smaller and smaller until the train entered the tunnel and sent me on the path back to my everyday life.

Until we see each other again.

ACKNOWLEDGMENTS

Thank you to all the readers, teachers, bookstore owners and workers, and librarians who supported my first book and made this second book possible; to my teaching colleagues who helped me through changing schools during a global pandemic, particularly Zac Carr, Cristina Veresan, Reenie Charrière, and Sabrina Garcia; to David Fullen and Jenn Bishop for their meticulous and extremely helpful feedback on the opening chapters; to Anika Hussain and the Young Editors Project for offering to read the first draft of this book, and to the many young editors whose notes immeasurably enhanced the characters—Ashley, Sydnee, Romilly, Cara, Corinne, Holly, Isabella, Ilaria, Teddy, and Will; to Thomas Trinh for traveling with me to a French farm and being a source of goodwill despite my many shifting moods; to my agent, Jim McCarthy, for continuing to support me and my writing alongside his very busy schedule; to Amy Cloud for helping carve a rounded story from my rough draft with her thoughtful notes and incisive cuts; to Erika West and Maxine Bartow for further clarifying the prose with detailed line edits; to Mallory Clinger for the beautiful cover art; to the rest of the production team at Clarion Books and HarperCollins for putting this book out there; to my sister Rachel, Aunt Wendy, and Grandpa Burke; and to Sanaz Talaifar for making my life better every day and always challenging me to think in new ways: I could not have written this book without you.